PLENTY

KELLY K. LAVENDER

Plenty
Copyright@ 2015 by Kelly K. Lavender

ISBN 978-0-9909431-2-9 EBOOK
ISBN 978-0-9909431-3-6 PRINT
LCCN # 2015907539

Published and Distributed by Kelly K. Lavender Press
Printed in the United States

ALL RIGHTS RESERVED. No part of this publication may be transmitted or reproduced or distributed in any form or by any means, electronic or mechanical, including photocopying, recording or by any information storage and retrieval system, without prior written permission from the publisher.

The characters and events portrayed in this book are fictitious. Any similarity to real persons, living or dead, is coincidental and not intended by the author.

Cover design by Damon Za
Formatting by Polgarus Studio

For more information about Kelly K. Lavender or her Multi-Award-Winning debut novel, *Beautiful Evil Winter*, visit www.kellyklavenderauthor.com.

Acknowledgements

Thanks to the peace officers that protect and serve, making our lives more peaceful and safe.

Thanks to DPS Trooper Jeanne Dark for sharing your time, valuable thoughts and observations during a three-hour long interview. By the way, Trooper Dark speaks to civic organizations, colleges and to students of all ages.

Thanks to my family for the wellspring of support.

Thanks to the many paramedics interviewed, I'm truly grateful for your time service, assistance and medical perspectives.

Thanks to the president of the local beekeepers club for the face-to-face encounter with wondrous all-important honeybees. Thanks also for answering my many questions.

Author's Note

As an equine addict, I have to warn horse owners not to place inquisitive unworldly foals or playful curious horses in close proximity to beehives. *As a rule, according to my research, bees have no interest in horses unless they disturb the hive, intentionally or not.* Horses co-exist peacefully with bees at our farm where they share a fence boundary covered with some honeysuckle vines. *Having said that, I would never put bee habitats in the same paddock as my horses.* Since horses like to use trees and stationary objects to scratch or crib, it's a good idea to check trees for bees and to place bee habitats away from horse paddocks. Since I don't claim to be an expert, I recommend that you contact a beekeeper and/or a veterinarian if you have any questions about a hive in or near a horse pasture.

Contents

Acknowledgements iii
Author's Note v

Chapter 1.   Cataclysm 1
Chapter 2.   Parasitism 14
Chapter 3.   Soul Searing 23
Chapter 4.   Mark 30
Chapter 5.   Joy 38
Chapter 6.   The Show 43
Chapter 7.   Relocation 48
Chapter 8.   Skills 55
Chapter 9.   Bee Seduced 62
Chapter 10.   Plans Interrupted 68
Chapter 11.   Grammy 75
Chapter 12.   Ben 82
Chapter 13.   The Bet 89
Chapter 14.   Eyes on the Target 96
Chapter 15.   Max 101
Chapter 16.   Bulletproof 113
Chapter 17.   Collateral Damage 121
Chapter 18.   Detectives 129

Chapter 19.	Jennifer's Day	136
Chapter 20.	Watley	144
Chapter 21.	The Discovery	151
Chapter 22.	Karma	158
Chapter 23.	The Epiphany	161
Chapter 24.	Bee Smart	164
Chapter 25.	The Dance	170
Chapter 26.	Going to the Dogs	178

Chapter 1
Cataclysm

The mesquite brush partially hid his presence. Standing armed, barefoot, and shirtless in the morning sun, he gazed east at the expanse of freeway that stretched in front of him. His ball cap and sunglasses did little to block the sun's glare. When he raised his left hand to add more shade, his TAC-338A shifted, prompting a smile. A playful touch from a lover not more inviting. He stroked the gun like a wanton man caressing a woman's curves. His dilated blue eyes, jittery hands, and jerky movements contrasted with the green camo pants of a serious hunter—his fully aroused body in jarring juxtaposition with the assigned task.

"Guns are like art. How can you not like guns?" he questioned rhetorically as he scratched his crotch. The morning sun warmed his fingers and glinted off his diamond rings. "Nope, can't have sparkle," he muttered aloud as he leaned his weapon against his late-model Toyota Corolla.

With a few pulls, he removed the jewelry, opened the car door, and placed it carefully in the console next to his flask. His fingers fluttered then lighted on the flask as a butterfly might flitter then settle on a flower. His eyes darted left and right as if he expected a slap on the hand before he tipped the container. After a quick glance at his watch, he cozied up to a bush near his car and peed on a flowering plant that managed to stretch toward the life-giving sun. Taking a moment to reflect after he zipped his fly, he reached into his front pocket for the wadded tissue used yesterday to wipe his bloody nose, a post-soiree necessity after indulging his insatiable appetite for blow. After one quick swipe to clear his nose, he dropped the tissue and stomped on it, enraged. Being a coke addict not what he'd planned for his life—but then again, neither was contract-killing specialist.

He grabbed his bipod and his rifle, gasping as if burned, before he cuddled his treasure to lie prone on the ground. Deeper breaths escaped his lips as he looked through his new $2,000 scope. The highway lay within range, just four hundred yards away. The brush provided perfect cover for his car and him. His target would be unmistakable—an old blue Ford truck, speckled with Bondo, pulling a flatbed. A scheduled drop would make the task easy. Purvis—too sloppy, too addicted, too stupid to be valuable . . . anymore. Nestling into a spot, the hit man grinned and sighted his gun on the highway in full view. He grimaced for a moment as he realized his hands still trembled.

I'm a little shaky, but I can hit a moving truck. After all, that's what hit men do.

***

A pearl-white Prius raced along the stretch of interstate for an important meeting, possibly life-changing for Camille.

"Wouldn't you rather own a Corvette? A Prius can't compare. I mean, there's no cool factor," Camille said as she fingered the fuzzy bee dangling beneath the rearview mirror.

"Well, actually I like Corvettes, but that car wouldn't be useful in my life now. As a church youth-group leader, I have to travel more than you'd imagine. Layer on the commute to town, and I'd put a hundred thousand miles on that car in no time," Mark answered with a smile. "Cool isn't always the priority, Camille."

"Maybe not when you're old, I guess," she mused. "You do listen to cool music. I like Queen. 'We Are the Champions' is by far one of my favorite songs. Crank it up!"

Mark adjusted his slumping posture to sit a little taller and turned the volume down. "I'm only thirty years old, Camille. My family hasn't prepared for my funeral yet." He continued, "Enough about me—let's talk about you."

"Whaaaaat now?" she said with a roll of her eyes as she placed her hands in her lap.

"I think you'll enjoy meeting this group of teens. They've made some bad life decisions, experienced challenges at home, and you, well . . . you've had a bad start but you've managed to survive to craft another day to create a promising future for yourself. You can reassure them and help them. And given the fact that you're nineteen years old, they'll look up to you as a cool adult," Mark preached.

"Yeah, maybe," Camille muttered before looking out the window. "So, do you consider me to be one of your wayward teens?"

"I think you've gotten a bad start and made a bad decision to become Grant's girlfriend. Given all of that, I think you'll tap into your personal power, and I hope to help you do that."

Camille turned her nose up and sniffed before she said, "By the way, you could improve the looks of this yawner car if you'd remove the bee and the white saddled horse attached to the dash. Are you competing for a nerd award? Most girls would think you could be hot if you let that brown hair grow a little longer and didn't dress like a senior citizen in khaki pants. Those green eyes of yours don't look old, so you still have a chance," Camille chuckled.

"I love bees and horses. You should learn more about them. Without bees, there would be no beautiful flowers in my home or fruits and vegetables to eat. Besides being a buffer against massive starvation on the planet, they fascinate me. The orange scent in the car serves as a reminder to me to be grateful for their presence. And horses—well, horses are the Great Healers and absolutely enchanting. I'd rather own a horse than a metal box powered by 450 horsepower—much cooler, for sure. The white horse reminds me of my vow to ride the white horse, to be a hero even in the smallest of ways."

"So, I'm your current project?" Camille questioned as she stared at the horse with a frown.

"Camille, just trust me here. You volunteered for the Youth Outreach Group at school; so, this interests you. You can actually help these girls, especially Violet. She's only fourteen years old and already pregnant."

"How sad!" Camille said, her frown deepening. Glancing away from the horse, she looked out the window. Ahead, a four-lane interstate, two lanes stretching east and two lanes west, separated by fifty yards of grassy median.

"What a beautiful, sunny morning! I'll just get in the slower right lane and coast along so we can savor it," Mark said as he checked his rearview mirror.

Camille stared as the vintage steel blue Ford truck crossed the centerline and then veered onto the right shoulder. "You'd better do something fast. That driver behind us must be drinking. He's all over the road," she said, biting her fingernail.

"Yeah, it looks like people are lining up behind me," Mark said as he floored the accelerator to pass with a wide margin into the left lane.

When Camille pivoted right and looked over her shoulder, she stared at the driver, who shook his head, blinked his vacant eyes, and shared his toothless smile with her. "That guy is impaired and pulling a flatbed of pallets. How insane is that?" she commented with a sneer.

Mark checked his rearview mirror to see the blue Ford truck move into the left lane and speed up.

"He's moved into the left lane. Looks like he plans to tailgate us, since he suddenly sped up," Camille mumbled before grabbing the overhead handhold attached to the ceiling.

"Hold on! I'm going back to the right lane. I bet he can't make a fast adjustment," Mark sputtered. "Someone let me over. Don't let him over, but let me over."

"I'll see if I can help." Camille motioned at the driver leading on the right. "Good, a guy." Waving like a cheerleader and pointing to the right, she managed to catch the driver's eye. With a quick smile and a flip of her black mane, she sealed the deal. "Okay, move. No signal needed. In fact, it would be a bad idea with that Bumpkin behind us."

After Mark moved over, Camille turned around, batted her violet eyes, and blew a thank-you kiss to the driver who let them pass.

"Whew! Better!" Mark said. "I wish I could warn other drivers."

"I think they can figure it out. I think I'd slow down enough to increase the distance between him and us, but not enough to encourage passing in front of us. That Bumpkin might try to side-slam them or us, causing a crash," Camille suggested.

"Yes, certainly," Mark agreed.

"Oh, no!" Camille shouted as she stared at the side mirror. "I think that red SUV behind him may try to pass him or us. It must be going ninety now. That woman doesn't understand. She's putting her family in danger." Looking at Mark, she said, "She just honked and swerved left. I see an old man ducking and covering his head with his hands."

Mark tightened his grip on the wheel before glancing side to side.

"About to inch beside us," Camille said, twisting left. "Good grief! There's a bullet hole spidering the front windshield between the driver and the old man! What the—?"

"Camille! Look around! Try to see where it came from!" Mark screeched.

"Really, Mark? What good will that do for us? Our immediate danger faces us on the asphalt, not off the asphalt. Nobody wants to shoot us. We're not that important," she said as she scanned the landscape before focusing on the family again. "There's a young girl in the backseat. She's ducking too, hands on her head, screaming and crying. That bullet *just* sliced through their car," Camille reasoned.

"And Bumpkin . . . Bumpkin just races along like nothing happened," Camille reported.

"Kind of nervous about those towers of pallets," Mark said.

"Crossing the centerline!" Camille yelled as Bumpkin swerved sharply left, sending a seemingly secure tower of pallets cascading toward the SUV.

With a quick crank of the steering wheel, the SUV skidded off the asphalt and rocketed onto the grassy median, avoiding the fallen heap.

"That SUV off the road, on the median. Now, headed back to the road," Camille updated Mark. "Back tires spinning, dirt clods flying. When they pop the underside of the car, they sound like bullets. Personal experience with my Corvette has taught me that. You have to fight physics for control."

"Oh, God! Out of control!" Camille screamed.

In a split second, the speeding SUV returned to the asphalt and reversed course, ricocheting like a missile launched across the grassy median and onto the westbound side, right into the path of an oncoming eighteen-wheeler. The screams of a family muffled by the skidding, smoking tires of a jackknifing truck as the startled truck driver tried to stop the carnage. The *BOOM* of two missiles colliding head-on at seventy miles per hour trumpeted the death of at least four people. As the eighteen-wheeler exploded, the smoke and flames of an oil-refinery blast reached upward to paint the blue sky black and gray. Broken glass and twisted metal spewed outward in multiple directions seeking a spot to embed, an atomic apocalyptic comment on the senseless tragedy.

The sounds of a normal day, shattered by the crunch of metal, shattered glass, screeching tires, and sobs from other drivers, now stopped. A fringe of faces, fighting shock, horror, and disbelief, grabbed cell phones while comforting loved ones who witnessed an unbelievable twist of fate——the annihilation of a family.

Mark pulled over the car and stared in silence as tears misted his eyes.

"What the hell?" Camille muttered, dazed. "They just died. I would've done the same thing she did. I didn't know the grass could send you to the other side. With a deep breath, she continued, "You never see that! You never think about that! We just saw the last seconds of their lives…In a flash, everyone died," Camille stammered, sadness veiling her face. "How would church explain that away?"

As Camille buried her face in her hands, sobbing, Mark reached over to rub her back.

"I can't go there now. My mind can only deal with this tragedy," Mark said. "My only question is …" he said, looking at the queue of cars in front of and behind them. "Where's the flatbed with the pallets?"

Drying her eyes on her sleeve, Camille twisted to find an

answer—once, then twice. "I can't see it." A sniffle later, she said, "Hey, I'll walk around outside to get a better look. Maybe I'll see him parked further up the road."

***

As Camille opened the door to the Prius, the scream of sirens filled the cabin.

"I heard someone say if all wheels returned to the road, the car would flip. Better to stay on the grassy median, even if it means hitting a tree or crashing into a ditch. And there's no one parked around here with a flatbed! I asked and searched. That person left or didn't know he lost pallets," she said.

"Get in, Camille. We'll make sure he knows!"

"Well, we don't know if he exited or is still headed east," Camille observed.

"We have to try. It's the right thing to do," Mark decided as he gripped the steering wheel.

An exit sign whizzed by as Mark drove with the fervor of a new father taking his wife to the delivery room. Finally, the flatbed came into view. The steel-blue Ford Ranger XLT moved erratically on the road, weaving left and right. Mark noticed that surrounding cars created a buffer zone around the truck.

"The only thing I can do is stay behind him and flash our lights, hoping that he'll see us. A single honk might help, too," Mark muttered.

"He could be high *and* drunk or sleep-deprived. Be careful!" Camille cautioned.

"Regardless, we have him in our sights. The cops aren't even close yet. Piecing the puzzle together and talking to witnesses take time. I bet this person is sleep-deprived. After all, it *is midmorning*, not late night," Mark deduced.

"Look, Bumpkin is waiving us along, inviting us to move up beside him. Do you think we should do that, Mark?" Camille questioned.

"I don't think I want to. He can't seem to stay in his lane. Let's wait and see if he stops somewhere up ahead. Actually, I think I saw a sign about a rest stop," Mark replied.

"Hey, you were right! There's a rest stop, and he's pulling over. Now, Mark, don't let rage cloud your judgment. Tell him in a helpful way," Camille coached.

With a roll of his eyes, Mark parked behind the flatbed, exited the car, and walked slowly to the waiting truck. Music from the truck filled the space between them. He angled his approach so as to be clearly seen, not suddenly in sight.

At the window, Mark spoke loudly, to be heard by the driver and Camille.

"Sir, I noticed some pallets slipped out of your truck. The SUV following behind you swerved to avoid them and ended up in a fatal wreck. I hope that they weren't following you, caravan style," Mark spoke in a slow, measured way as he looked into the cab.

Camille noticed the bearded man behind the wheel didn't meet Mark's eyes, but he did turn off the radio. When he finally faced Mark, Camille suspected his eyes were dilated, from the way he squinted. His mouth, a dark crevice lined with charred stumps for teeth, snarled like a cheetah disturbed.

When Camille saw Mark take an awkward step backward, she put her hand on the car horn and craned her neck, waiting for a sign to interrupt to change the subject.

"Well, as long as you know, I'll be on my way," she heard Mark say.

"Just a minute," the driver croaked. "I don't like to be followed.

What are you, a vigil . . . ante?"

"No, I think of myself as a Good Samaritan. I apologize for following you, for trying to get your attention," Mark reassured.

"Apology accepted," Mr. Bumpkin said as he focused on the front windshield again.

Camille watched Mark's gaze wander to the lock of Bumpkin's hands on the steering wheel and the flex of his jaw. "Well, I'll be on my way, sir." As Mark turned away and began walking back to the car, he saw Camille approaching. "No!" Mark mouthed as he nodded his head.

"Okay, all is well," she acknowledged.

As she closed her car door, her questioning eyes searched Mark's face.

"What a scary son of a bitch! I think he's on drugs—something requiring a pipe." Mark said, refusing to meet her eyes. "I saw a small pipe resting in the ashtray."

"How did it end?"

"All right, I think. He acted like he was a few steps behind the world around him. Let's leave." Mark hesitated a few seconds before pulling a Taser from the center console and securing it under his seat. "Self-defense and protecting my family are always on my mind," he mumbled.

"Oh my gosh!" Camille cried out. "Why would he circle his rig around to our car? It looks like *crack-smoking* Bumpkin wants to talk to you."

While the driver lowered his window, Mark sat transfixed, then mimicked his actions.

"I knew I dropped part of my load. It's not easy to push out of the line of traffic. Didn't know anyone would die over it. I guess when your number is up, it's up," he smiled. "Anyway, it's time to forget that you met me. Mind your own business!" Bumpkin hissed.

"Yes, sir. We'll be on our way," Mark replied with upmost respect. When his face turned red and he gripped the gearshift, Camille knew he was struggling to conquer the fire-breathing dragon of fury that threatened to take control. She had fought that battle many times. His jaw flexed and relaxed in an instant, which caused Camille to wonder exactly what he would do to avert trouble.

"Don't speed away. In his state of mind, he may treat us like prey," Camille whispered under her breath, careful to look straight ahead.

Camille stared into the side mirror. She saw Bumpkin's head dip and reappear. When he exited his car, facing away from them with his hands positioned in front of him as if to urinate, Camille said, "Bumpkin's out of the car. I'm worried. There's only ten feet separating us. Go!"

Spinning around so fast that he almost fell, Bumpkin smiled and trained his Glock on Mark.

"He has a gun pointed at us! Step on it!" Camille screamed.

Bumpkin blinked before he fired, and Mark fell. The Prius veered sharply right until Camille grabbed the wheel. Screaming Camille covered Mark's body, now sprawled over the console. Blood and gray brain matter splattered the black leather steering wheel, black dash, and the white horse.

"NO! NO!" Camille shrieked hysterically.

As the next shot rang out, Mark's body jumped as it absorbed the bullet.

Camille moved away from his lifeless body and assumed a fetal position, wedged between the seat and floorboard. Her hands trembled as she clasped them behind her neck to hide her head from the shooter's view.

The ensuing silence seemed insufferable. Her thoughts raced. *Can't push him out of the car without letting Bumpkin know I'm alive.*

Even if I could move into his seat, Bumpkin can shoot me before I can blink. Can I move his upper body only then move his legs to push the accelerator rather than the brake? She risked a peek at the side-view mirror.

Bumpkin lumbered toward the Prius for the kill shot, his gun dangling from his right hand.

She positioned herself sideways in the passenger seat, hunched down, and used her legs to push Mark off the console to get to the Taser under his seat. She heard a *click* of the door lock as she made a final effort. Shuddering, she refused to look at the door, as if he would go away as a result.

Tap, tap. When he tapped on the glass, leering at her with that deep, dark well of a smile, she submissively lowered the window. Her eyes darted back and forth as she struggled for a plan to escape.

"I see that pretty face trying to figure out what's in store for you. Just remember, if you try anything, I'm an expert shot with either hand."

Camille felt the wet warmth of urine, like blood, between her legs.

"Well, your partner's number was up today, ma'am. My aim was good, so he didn't suffer," Bumpkin said, staring at the body.

"I'm glad you made me come to you, because I like the ladies, especially the pretty ones like you." His smile widened, a few cigarette-butt-sized stubs of white peeking through. He leaned into the open window space. "Yummm…, I like you and your lily-white skin, that black hair, those violet eyes." He ogled her while his hand reached out and grazed her breast.

"You disgust me!" she spat.

"Now, unlock the door and let me in!" he growled. "Push it open for me. I want to get closer to you, darling," he coaxed.

"Okay, you win!" Camille shouted. "Done!" She glared as he invaded her personal space.

He smiled again, his mouth like a wildfire disaster scene in a once-wooded area—now only a few charred white birch surviving.

Grabbing her arm, he roughly yanked her out of the car. As she resisted, he laughed, tightening his grip.

"I'm taking you with me to my truck," he crowed.

"No!" Camille shouted as she stomped on his instep and elbowed him in the gut. A quick release—enough time for her to run.

"Yes!" he shouted as he lunged for her, grabbing a fistful of her long hair. "You going to cooperate, Princess, or am I going to have to shoot you here?" Dragging her toward him with a rope of hair, he locked his arm and elbow across her chest. She dug her heels into the asphalt to slow his march.

"Now, when we get to my truck, you get in like a good girl. 'Cause if you don't, I'll take your head off with a single shot, just like your partner. Got it, Princess?"

At the driver's door, he released her momentarily and shoved her into the cab, scooting in beside her on the bench seat.

"Now, give me some sugar, Princess," he said as he leaned into her, grabbing her breast.

"Fuck you!" she shrieked, punching him with the rapidity of a prizefighter.

"I'm glad you want that. I'd like that with your mouth, right here, right now," he demanded.

His right arm formed a triangle around her neck to restrain her. As he fumbled to start the car, Camille elbowed him and battered him with her right fist.

***

That's when *it h*appened. A shot rang out. The bullet dropped Bumpkin like a deer. The barefoot, shirtless sniper, lying prone, leaned to the right away from his gun and laughed, his weapon never used.

Chapter 2
Parasitism

Grant usually wasn't on the road this early, but today an opportunity to see a special car, a black Camaro with lime-green racing stripes, lured the snoozer out of bed. As he zipped through the traffic, he slowed at the sight of the EMS vehicles and police cars. Traffic completely stopped on the westbound side as a wrecker hoisted a pancake-thin scrap of a car up and away. A queue of grieving mourners on the eastbound side confirmed the gruesomeness of the scene. Moving slowly along, he took note of the pallets and eased over to the shoulder. Grabbing his cell phone, he pushed a single button.

"Hey, we have a problem here on the main highway, I-20. Yeah, the drug alleyway. You probably want to check it out." Grant frowned as he listened, irritation fueling his response. "I'm here because I'm going to see a car further down the road." He rolled his eyes as the conversation continued. "Given all the accidents that happen on this freeway, I'd think that you'd want me buzzing around here on a daily basis. Besides, it's the only way to find great eats, go to a cool club, go to a professional football game or the shopping mall, all of which interest *me*. Unlike you, I like to go places where I can spend my stash of cash." Listening again, he nodded his head in frustration. "I can't wait for you. Got to see a car further down the road. We'll talk later."

After pocketing his phone, he rocketed away, leaving a spray of gravel in his wake. His blue BMW bike ripped along the road with urgency until he saw a man at a rest stop apparently dragging a woman to his truck. With a quick change into the left lane, he used the turnaround to get a closer look.

He inched up on the scene, parking his bike underneath a tree, away from the parking lot. As he crept along, he heard a man laughing. His eyes zeroed in on the single bullet hole and the blood splatter on the windshield of a Prius, and the body slumped over the console. *No one else in the car.* Grant crossed himself as he continued to walk. Heat surged through his veins as indignation bubbled up with volcanic force. His gaze settled on the truck. The woman clawed and punched at the man holding her by her hair.

"I'll kill you or die before you—!"

Grant pulled off his helmet, grabbed a gun from his waistband and fired.

"Oh my God!" Camille screamed as Bumpkin slumped onto the dashboard.

"Yes!" Grant shouted with a fist pump. He stashed his weapon and walked slowly to the car. "Let me help you."

Camille wailed and coughed, "Need help. He killed my friend, Mark. Mark shouldn't be dead. This stoner sexually assaulted me," she said as she sneered and scooted to the passenger door.

"I'll call for help," he told her while dialing his cell phone. Shaking his head in disgust, he added, "You can ride to the police station with me so you don't have to be part of this crime scene any longer."

"Okay," Camille whimpered.

As usual, she felt the grip of numb withdrawal take hold before she could react. Daring to gaze down at her trembling arms coated in blood and brains, tears threatened again. She looked into his eyes and saw the sadness that she felt.

"I want to go to the bathroom first to clean my arms and towel off my clothes."

"Okay, my dad will be here in about twenty minutes; then, we can go," Grant said soothingly.

Camille walked into the clean rest-stop bathroom. Never had she thought of an ample supply of soap and paper towels as a gift. She pushed the soap dispenser a couple of times with her elbow to extract a few drops of the honey-colored goo. Using her finger, she painted the soap onto her arms and face to clean away blood and splatter; afterwards, she cupped her hands under the faucet for a quick rinse. Next, she had to deal with her urine-soaked shorts. As she walked past the sinks, she grabbed a handful of paper towels, wet a few, and dotted them with soap. In the stall, she scrubbed her legs and spot-cleaned the shorts by dipping them in the just-flushed toilet. With the unused towels, she dried her shorts as much as possible.

He saw her surprise when she spotted him standing behind her at the mirror. He was the Good Samaritan, but he'd rather be known as Camille's beau.

Camille gasped as he pulled away his helmet. She could see his brown hair and soulful blue eyes. Her heart raced as she felt his breath play upon her hair.

"All better?" he asked as he wrapped his arms around her and breathed into her hair.

She likes this. She tells me it always makes her heart race. I'm her man candy, her coke.

"What took you so long? You're my knight in shining armor," she asked.

"I know this isn't the best time, but I won't take long. I promise," he said with a dark chuckle as he grabbed her ass. After he pulled her next to him, he positioned her on the counter to continue.

"You're my ddd . . . rug, Grant. Of all the guys I've ever known, I'm . . . your bitch," she stammered as she clawed at his back.

"Yeah, you're my girl, my first. You need this today to remind you that I own you," he said as his breathing slowed. "Time to be giddy, wild, and reckless for me, Camille."

***

When Grant squeezed his eyes shut for one more moment of ecstasy, he heard a deep resonating baritone voice rise above his grunts and sigh of release.

"Son, what have I told you about screwing the help? Now, zip up your pants and be on your way."

"D . . . ad, I'm a grown man. I'm almost finished here."

"Go on, Grant. Remember, I'm the law here."

As Grant stumbled out of the stall, pulling up his pants, Camille scrambled to make herself presentable.

When Camille exited the stall, Gordon grabbed her arm as she walked by him. After pointing his finger in her face, Gordon made his message clear.

"Now, Camille, you leave my son alone. We've talked about this. He's not some hillbilly bible-thumping gambler like that dumb ass guy in the Prius."

"You're coming with me to the police station to file a report. Let's go!" he ordered. As he grabbed her bicep, she winced in pain.

***

When Gordon steered his car into an empty barn, Camille shuddered with fear.

Grabbing her roughly by the arm, he pulled her out of the car, shoving her onto the ground. As she tried to regain her footing and upright herself, Gordon's closed fist struck her face.

"Stop! Don't beat me! I'll give you what you want!" Camille cowered, crying as blood trickled from her mouth.

He hovered over her like a wolf watching its next meal struggle.

"That's more like it, you slut. Let's see why sonny boy thinks you're so special." He crowed as he tore at her pants.

A moment of silence interrupted Gordon's grunting as he wrestled with her stuck zipper. The pause that followed deafening as she waited for the next blow.

"Forget it! You're just nasty! A re-homed girl living a loser life. Who knows what kind of germs you picked up along the way— probably crabs," he sneered. "I don't see what he sees in you. Camille with her stovepipe calves and veiny hands. Lucky you have that long black hair to cover your moose ears. He can do better. Zip your pants and get into the back of the car," Gordon ordered.

After Gordon settled into the front seat, he opened the glove box, and grabbed a bottle of antibacterial hand cleaner. While watching her wide-eyed, watery stare in the rearview mirror, he made a point of holding his hands high so she could see him disinfect them.

"Yep, that son of mine has a lot to learn. He's out of your league."

As she buried her head in her hands, he started the car and drove away back into town.

***

The headlines in the *Prosperity Picayune* read "Mark Jones, community leader, murdered on I-90. Police asking for information." On the same page, a picture of a jackknifed eighteen-wheeler with the caption, "Family dies in explosive crash. According to family members, the teenage victim planned to meet with Mark Jones to discuss placement of her unborn child."

Camille wiped away a tear as she thought of that horrible day—the wreck, Mark's death, and Gordon. She set the paper aside and buried her head in her arms on the kitchen table at her grandmother's house, which had been willed to her. It was springtime, April, her favorite time of year. The sultry breeze and song of the chirping birds trickling through the open windows did nothing to lift her spirit.

"Grammy, I need you so much. I don't know what to do," she wailed.

After dinner, rehearsing her words for effect, she called Grant. "Grant, I want to see you tonight, to talk to you tonight."

"Sweetie, I miss that luscious body of yours."

"Grant, we need to talk, that accident, Mark's death, that Bumpkin and your dad. Grant, he . . . hurt . . . me. I can't clear my head. I'm so sad," Camille sniffled.

"Baby, I'll be right over; just wait for me."

"Gordon doesn't want you to treat me nice. He doesn't want us to care about one another," she whined.

"You take care of me, and I'll take care of my dad. I promise," he cooed.

When Grant walked through the screen door, Camille felt the flutter of butterflies in her bosom and a bonfire building in her crotch. She ran across the room to him and cradled the sides of his face for a kiss while pressing her body into his arousal. His scent, a mix of pine and musk, always made her ravenous—a hungry cheetah stalking an injured antelope could not be more intense.

"I'm so sad, Grant. I need you so much. Hold me, Grant. Help me get over this."

With a gentle motion, Grant pulled her hands away from his face and looked at her pleading, watery eyes.

"First, things first, baby. Do me. Don't kiss my mouth. Take me in your mouth. I can't concentrate with this baseball bat between my legs. I told you how much it hurts when you don't satisfy me—it's like having a pincushion between my legs. Blow me, baby."

"I understand. You must be in terrible pain." With a blink of her eyes, a deep breath, and a shrug of her shoulders, she pushed him against the wall and unzipped his fly. When his pants fell around his ankles, he stepped out of them, kicked off his shoes, and closed the distance between them.

Grant arched his back into her full lips while grabbing fistfuls of her black, silky mane. Pulling her head closer into his body, he groaned.

"Look at me with those beautiful violet eyes while you're sucking me! Now, Camille! Yes . . . so good," Grant mumbled. "Stand up, Camille. Face me," Grant croaked as he tore at the front of her shirt. "Unhook that bra and let it fall, Camille. Strip for me."

With a sigh and roll of her eyes, she stepped back a few steps twirled around slowly, tossed her bra and unbuttoned her skirt. When it lay in a heap on the floor, she kicked it to the side, rearranged her hair to cover her breasts, and beckoned him toward her with her hands and her parted pouty lips, just as he had taught her.

Grant licked his lips as he moved toward her with his baseball bat in hand.

Her eyes darted to the window when she heard the crunch of gravel outside.

"Did you hear that?" she froze.

"Hear what?" he smiled as he continued toward her.

Camille turned to run to another room of the house when Grant grabbed her from behind and pushed her into her grandmother's bedroom.

"Not here! My room! I don't want to soil my Grammy's room. I want to keep it the way she left it."

"Camille, it's my way, baby. Always, on my terms, darling," Grant said as he shoved her onto the bed.

As she scrambled to get away, he grabbed her panties, tearing them away. Still skittering, Camille angled toward the headboard and the lamp sitting nearby on the nightstand. Lunging at her, Grant grabbed her foot and pulled her butt underneath him.

"You're fun. Sometimes you're my ho, and sometimes you act like you don't want it. No problem, baby, I don't mind working for it," he said as pulled her legs apart, pushed down on her lower back, and plunged into her.

"No, Grant. Not this time, not here," Camille begged.

"Oh, baby, quit whining. Go with it," he coached as his hand explored her crotch.

"Stop, Grant," she muttered as she melted into him, her breathing suddenly loud and raspy.

"That's what I'm talking about! Screw me, baby!" Grant cried out as he fondled her breasts.

"Now, to take it up a notch." Grant pulled the covers away, twisted to the side, and plucked a syringe hidden inside his white tube sock.

"There, there, Darling, a little heroin and it's all better now. Just roll with it," he cajoled as he jabbed the needle into her calf and buried himself deeply over and over again.

"So good, Grant. Always so great," she purred before she passed out.

With a smile, Grant grazed his hand along Camille's ass and nuzzled his face in her disheveled mane, breathing in her honeysuckle scent.

The creak of the wood floor triggered a frown, interrupting his conquistador moment. As he glanced at the bedroom doorway, the glint of a badge caught his eye.

Chapter 3
Soul Searing

Grant stared at his dad's exuberant chimpanzee smile for a few moments before he rolled away from unconscious Camille and pulled up his pants. Before the final zip and snap, he glanced at his dad and back at Camille again.

He's so disgusting, but he is my dad. He beats me, he scolds me, he controls me, and I hate him for it! I hate what he does with his life!

"Time for you to go, son. We'll handle this from here," Gordon said.

As Gordon stepped aside to let him pass, he noticed Bruce, the town mayor, don a mask before he thrust a wad of cash into his dad's hand.

"By the way, son, we'll make some money on that footage. Your daddy is so proud of you."

***

Camille awoke naked, staring at the ceiling. Although groggy and sore, her thoughts drifted to her beloved Grammy's bed, now tainted by sex and Grant's selfish behavior. She glanced at the Bible that rested on the nightstand.

Nobody's perfect. Only God is perfect, she reminded herself as she rose and slid across the sticky sheets.

With a shrug of her shoulders and a smile, she grabbed her shredded green underwear off the floor as she made her way to the shower. The blue fingerprints around her wrist brought another smile to her lips as she recalled how passionate she and Grant were behind closed doors. She noticed more bruises in the shower as she soaped her thighs. Camille winced as the horrible scent of pine disinfectant and pencil shavings assailed her nose. *Grant's new aftershave is revolting! Screwing in Grammy's room worse, disgusting!*

Tears streamed from her eyes as her thoughts drifted to her grandma.

Grammy believed in me. Believed that I'd be special and strong. She told me to pursue a meaningful life. Look at me—drugging recreationally and balling my boyfriend in her bed. So unhappy and so ashamed of my weakness. Where did I go wrong to create this train wreck of a life?

Before she fell asleep that night, Camille remembered her vow to drive to nearby Nickel to meet Mark's friends and family. Tomorrow, she'd keep that promise to herself.

***

Meanwhile, Gordon cackled as he watched her shower from his cushy couch.

"Yeah! This is the best footage I've seen."

"Yes, Bruce, this girl is a moneymaker for sure."

After a *clink* of their longnecks, Gordon hit the rewind button.

***

The sun peeked over the horizon, and the trees and green grass blurred as Camille raced along the open road in her red vintage

Corvette Stingray. After all, there were advantages to being Grant's girl, she could speed in the car her grandmother gave her. *Gordon and Grant always had more important tasks than watching her every move.* She pressed the accelerator, savoring the growl of the engine and the adrenaline rush as it pounced, then charged ahead like a lioness chasing a gazelle. She rarely listened to music when driving. Like her Grammy, she was a gear girl. Like her grandmother, Mobil One motor oil, not blood, streamed through her veins.

"These stupid damn unsafe trucks from Mexico turning off the highway to travel 64 to Prosperity!" she growled, slapping the steering wheel.

Nickel waited a few miles ahead. Nickel, a one-stoplight town with a busy truck stop and a Rainbow bread factory, boasted "Clean Country Life at Its Best" via the faded sign bordering the city limits. Like a foal stumbling to gain its footing, Nickel still hadn't gained the ability to gallop along at stopwatch speed like Prosperity.

"There's that church Grandma loved," Camille muttered to herself as she lowered her window in the hope that the scent of mouthwatering freshly baked bread would waft her way.

***

Camille's thoughts turned to that day—the day of her grandmother's funeral at Nickel United Methodist Church six months ago.

Mourners poured through the white five-picket gate like a can't-be-contained swollen stream. The white steeple framed a beautiful sun-shaped mosaic in stained glass depicting Jesus reaching out to his followers. The white picket fence surrounding the church added to the postcard-perfect picture.

Mark, the youth-group minister, and his wife, Jennifer, sat beside

Camille to hold her hand and offer a shoulder to cry on, as a pillar of support and strength. Others sat and wept for their own loss, not bothering to comfort Camille, Barbara's rebellious granddaughter and only living relative.

"I didn't realize how many people loved her as much as I did," Camille bawled, leaning on Jennifer's shoulder.

"She loved you dearly, Camille. She told us one day you'd surprise all of us in some special way. Nothing made her light up like you did," Jennifer soothed. "We know you'll do something good with your life to honor her and yourself."

"Are her friends too good to talk to me? What's that, anyway? Hypocrisy or a snub?" Camille asked.

"Forgive them. Everyone grieves differently. Situations aren't always what they seem. Remember that, Camille. Don't be too trusting or too distrusting."

"Darling Camille," Angie said, grabbing Camille's hand. The cloud of gardenia cologne enveloped them as they embraced.

"Dear, sweet Angie. You know my grandmother loved you—you were her best friend. Are you going to be okay?"

"How lovely of you to think about me at a time like this! You know I'm only a phone call away if you need anything. And remember, I'm just one street away from Barbara's house, now your house."

"Promise me you'll get your GED, no matter what happens. Barbara would want you to do that."

"I promise I'll do it online. I don't want to go back to school and be the pitiful one. Everyone seems to know about my parents already. My loser dad, in prison for distributing porn, and my meth-addict mom, who ran out onto the freeway to commit suicide courtesy of speeding cars. What a bunch of losers! They treated Grammy so mean, and she supported them. Honestly, she took care of them and me," Camille said.

"Remember—it's not what you have, it's what you do with what you have. Honor her by rising above your situation."

"Okay, Angie. Thanks for the sermon," Camille said to end the conversation. She rolled her eyes and sat stone-faced for the rest of the service.

Later, the church was quiet as Camille sat alone with the coffin of her grandmother. A few moments asked for, a few moments granted, before Mark and others loaded the hearse.

Streams of mascara-black tears soaked the collar of her blouse and burned her already red eyes.

"Grammy, I don't know what to do without you! I'm so ashamed of my parents! I wish they were better people for both of us! I apologize for the way they treated you, mistreated you. I wish I could've done more to protect you!" Camille wailed as she lay over the casket.

After the last mourner left the gravesite, she heard the roar of a motorcycle. Grant appeared by her side in all of his glory, clean-shaven and sprinkled with cologne.

"No more tears, baby," he remarked as he sat next to her.

Camille rested her head on his shoulder as she dabbed her nonstop tears with a Kleenex.

Gently, he turned her chin toward his face.

"It's officially over. She's dead. Time to move on. Let's make some noise tonight! Chase away those tears!"

"I don't want to screw you tonight, Grant."

"Let's go to your house—that sounds weird, but it's now legally your house—and hang out together. Do you really want to be alone tonight?" he cajoled. "I've got something that will lighten your spirits. Hop on my bike. Let's go!"

"All right, you win. But no sex," Camille stated.

***

A shard of light pierced the darkness settling in the kitchen. The ethereal sunset held all the promise of restful, spiritual rejuvenation—a time to reflect on Grammy's goodness and think about the next step.

The TV cast light in the darkened living room as Camille's favorite movie, *Titanic*, tore at her heartstrings.

"Here you go, darling. One sweet tea for you and a Pepsi for me," Grant offered as he sat next to her on the couch.

When Camille slumped against his shoulder, Grant scooped her up.

The light from the sun warmed her skin, awakening her. With a start, she realized that she was back in her Grammy's bed. Her thoughts ran wild as she checked for clothing and signs. *That dog is gone, and I'm naked—the smells of sex smeared on my skin. He had sex with me! I must have been stoned to have no memory of that!*

***

The next day, Grant appeared on her doorstep, dressed to kill in khaki shorts and a navy-blue Polo top, and held out a peace offering of pink daisies.

"I'm so sorry, Camille. So selfish of me. I can't control myself around you. My crotch reacts to you, and it hurts until I get some satisfaction. All roads lead back to you. You're so beautiful."

"I have to forgive you. I guess I understand since it's difficult to control myself around you, too," she said with a small smile as she stood in the doorway in a yellow rose-patterned skirt and top.

When he leaned in for a kiss, he grabbed her ass and pulled her toward him as he maneuvered her back into the house. With a kick, he slammed the door shut behind them.

"You're insatiable!" she giggled.

"One more time. You smell so clean and sweet," Grant cooed as his hand parted her thighs, pushed up under her skirt, and pulled her bluebonnet bikini panties to one side. "Just go with it, baby! This one's for you," he croaked as he dropped to his knees.

As his motorcycle roared away from her driveway, Camille stepped into the shower to wash away the guilt, the self-loathing, and all traces of him.

Chapter 4
Mark

Camille parked her car in front of the church and waited for Mark's widow, Jennifer, to arrive. A spring rain glazed the streets, mixing with the scent of freshly baked bread and creating a euphoric olfactory experience. Camille leaned back against her seat and lowered both windows to increase the flow of succulent smells. Inhaling deeply and rhythmically, she savored the moment and its simplicity, wiggling her pink-painted toes in delight.

This is as good as reefer she mused as watched the passing cars.

A maroon minivan pulled into the parking lot, stopping next to her Stingray. Jennifer stared at her steering wheel for a few minutes before meeting Camille's eyes with a tearful gaze.

"Why don't you come to my house so we can visit? Or would you prefer to be more public about our conversation? I know you must have some questions for me, too," Jennifer said as she leaned into the open window.

"Sure. I'd rather talk to you one-on-one without worrying about some churchgoing hypocrite interrupting us. Too many of those folks leave their Christian faith at the church on Sunday after the service," Camille answered.

Jennifer winced at these words, but motioned her hand toward the passenger door in invitation.

As they settled into the van and began their journey, silence polluted the cabin space.

"I apologize for not attending Mark's funeral last month. I wanted to, but I hate the people—the same small-minded, judgmental people that attended Grammy's funeral."

"Mark attended your grandmother's funeral," Jennifer reminded her quietly as she clutched the wheel tightly. "Do you think he was small-minded and judgmental?"

"No, Mark was different. He seemed to care about me. He treated me with respect and dignity. I didn't feel like a burden or a sex kitten around him," Camille said.

"He was a special man—caring, loving, and kind. Leading the youth group always gave him great joy. He cared about you, worried about you just like your grandmother did," Jennifer reflected.

"Did my grandmother talk to him about me?" Camille asked

"No, he never mentioned it to me. Mark did notice that you weren't interested in anyone but Grant, and didn't want to spend time with anyone else," Jennifer said.

With a roll of her eyes, Camille turned toward the passenger window, staring at the trees, houses, horses, and round bales whizzing by.

"He thought you were very unhappy and headed for trouble. He noticed your grandmother change, too, from a happy, gentle soul to a worried wreck of a human being," Jennifer stated.

Camille slumped in her seat and leaned into the window while she dabbed at her watery eyes.

"I thought you had questions about Mark," Camille snapped.

"Yes, Mark was a special, unique, kind man—a wonderful husband and more," Jennifer sniffled.

***

"Here we are—home," Jennifer announced as she parked the minivan in front of a simple, white, two-story home, made more inviting by a wraparound porch with a bench swing near the front door.

Camille exited the car and marveled at the grazing horses, the meadow of orange and yellow wildflowers, and the rows of round bales resting like giant rollers ready for styling. Red roses and gardenias fringed the perimeter of the house, and two pink crepe myrtles stood like pillars on either side of the concrete steps leading to the front porch. Dark pink bougainvillea in pine-green plastic planters hung from precisely spaced hooks along the front and sides of the porch ceiling.

"Please come in," Jennifer gestured.

Camille took a moment to gaze at the beauty around her and inhale the perfume produced by the prospering plants surrounding her.

"So beautiful. It looks like a floral shop."

"A labor of love long in process. Mark, Joy, and I tend to them because they give us so much pleasure."

"Who's Joy?" Camille froze mid-step.

"Joy is our thirteen-year-old daughter. These lovely flowers pale in comparison to her. She means everything to me."

"Oh!" Camille murmured as she stepped onto the green woven circular rug, looking down as if to study every coil.

When she raised her eyes to meet the room, she noticed crystal bud vases filled with fresh flowers dotting the living room and kitchen area. Blue, brown and green earth tones appeared everywhere, from the afghan resting on the leather sofa to the pictures of saddled horses displayed on the walls. Shiny wood floors and the quiet whisper of a ceiling fan added warmth to the chocolaty-sweet setting.

"Your home is special—clean, happy, and full of color. I'll trade with you," Camille commented with a smile.

"No, I may sell it at some point, but Joy wants to stay here. We landscaped it ourselves. Joy even placed the bricks around the flowerbeds. Mark's dad, Richey, actually built the house after he married Mark's mom. My dad crafted the kitchen cabinets and built-in bookshelves and added the front porch swing. Of course, the bees are part of our legacy from Mark's family."

"Bees?" Camille asked.

"Yep, we sell honey, and the bees pollinate our flowers. Mark used the honey for gifts and to establish relationships. Joy is already expert at dealing with the bees. Her bee suit hangs on her closet-door hook so she can see it every morning when she wakes up. She even personalized it with pink flowers," Jennifer said with a smile. She paused in reflection, then walked to the living room floor-to-ceiling window.

Camille saw a couple of short squat white filing cabinets between the house and hay meadow. The long branch of a tree positioned outside the cross fencing marked the separation of the woods from both the bee town and the pastured horses.

"Mark always said, 'When you think you can't fly, remember the bees with their tiny wings and bulbous bodies,'" Jennifer reminisced. Gazing out the window, she asked, "Did you happen to notice his gold ring? He wore it as a wedding ring. It was a diamond cross ring customized with four tiny emeralds, one at each endpoint. Green was his favorite color."

"Y . . . es. I remember him wearing it that day, on his wedding ring finger. It's eye-catching. You have it, don't you?" Camille asked.

"Nooo—" Jennifer stammered.

"I promise I didn't take it!" Camille interrupted.

"I don't think that. I just wish I knew who did. I want it back for Joy. She adored her dad," Jennifer muttered, wiping away tears with the back of her hand. Without meeting Camille's gaze, she walked to face the window and grabbed a fistful of curtain for support.

"He always seemed like a perfect person to me," Camille consoled.

"No, he liked to gamble, at one point at the casino tables, and later, on people. He could be impulsive, brash, and too trusting. No, he wasn't a perfect person, but he always treated us with kindness and respect, like we were gifts of perfection blessing his life. He always made me feel honored and adored. Before Mark, the bad boys attracted me. I guess you could say I was the all-American cheerleader gone bad and gone good again. I never thought about it until now, but maybe he rescued me from myself, like the kids in the youth group."

"It's hard to believe there are guys like him out there. I trusted your husband. Never met anyone like him in my life. That day, he planned to take me to a place to meet some teen girls who had lost their parents like I did. He always told me to grow my world, to make more friends," Camille said in a whispery tone.

"If you thought he was so wonderful, why didn't I see you at the funeral or at the cemetery? Why?" she pressed. "Don't you think I'd want to talk to the last person to see my husband alive—the person who witnessed my husband's last breath? The person that he spoke so often of, the person he most wanted to help? The person who could best help me understand the life-changing events of that day?" Letting the curtain fall from her grasp, she faced Camille, her countenance encrypted with rage, hate, and deep-rooted sadness.

"I apologize. I hardly know what to say," Camille replied, casting her eyes at the floor as searing flames of shame engulfed her. "It was selfish and irresponsible."

"That begins to scratch the surface," Jennifer snarled. "So, why didn't you show up?"

Thoughts of that day flooded Camille's memory. She considered attending the funeral, but then she didn't go—not because she didn't want to but because she didn't want to deal with the same small-minded, judgmental hypocrites who had attended her grandmother's funeral. Besides, Grant wanted her to go to the lake to meet some of his motorcycle buddies, which wasn't fun since she was the only girl in the group. She crashed in the sun after a joint, the pill, and the longneck. She heard the guys howling as she fell face-first into the sand.

"I spent the day at the lake with Grant and his friends," Camille said, avoiding Jennifer's eyes.

"How can you sleep at night? You chose a beach party with a bunch of parasites rather than paying final respects to someone who tried to help you find happiness and a better path. What's wrong with this picture?" Jennifer asked.

"Grant isn't a parasite!"

"I've known about Grant for a while through youth-group chatter. He's no angel. He treats girls like commodities. Don't you see that?"

"What are commodities?"

"Commodities are goods to be used or exchanged."

"I never saw that in him," Camille rebutted.

"Does he ever treat you with kindness and respect like Mark did? Does he remind you of Mark in any way?" Jennifer questioned.

"People are different. People interact differently with people in their lives," Camille replied.

"Think about his character and not his face or what's under his zipper. You have to look beyond those superficial markers. Is he a good person? When the looks fade, what will you have left?" Jennifer asked.

Shaking her head, Camille stared at the floor. "You just don't understand."

"I understand more than you do. Prove me wrong and take a closer look. That's all I ask," Jennifer said.

Camille met Jennifer's gaze while wringing her hands. "So, what do you want to know about that day?"

"What happened that day? I just have bits and pieces of information."

"Your husband tried to do the right thing when that Bumpkin shot him. He tried to make the guy aware that his pallets had bounced from the truck to prevent more accidents that day."

"Why didn't he shoot you? You saw what happened."

"I . . . I believe it was just timing or dumb luck. Grant showed up on the scene. Bumpkin gave me a break because he…he wanted sexual favors from me. I fought him," Camille said, popping her knuckles.

"Did he take the ring?" Jennifer asked without judgment.

"No, I didn't see him take it."

"Did he die quickly?"

"Yes, he didn't expect to be shot. It was sudden and quick."

Jennifer clutched the curtains as her mouth became a hard line of hate. "He didn't believe that stretch of highway was dangerous," she said as she continued to stare outside. "He didn't believe that area was a drug corridor, a hot spot for consumers and suppliers. I've heard about it for years."

"Maybe, someone will return it," Camille chirped.

"No, I think I know who has it. It won't be returned. Some people have no moral code."

"Like who? An EMT, the mayor, or . . . a passerby, or . . . a dirty cop?" Camille contemplated, tapping her forefinger on her lips. "Maybe one of Gordon's officers—or Gordon!"

When Jennifer turned to face her with a savage stare, Camille knew she had reached a precipice of truth.

"Well, Jennifer, I might be able to help you with that! Yes, I definitely think I can."

Chapter 5
Joy

"Wake up, Joy," Jennifer called out. "It's already ten o'clock, and we have to deliver honey today."

Joy blinked her eyes and threw the covers aside and vaulted out of bed. Standing up, she stomped her feet to give the illusion of movement while she yawned and stretched her arms toward the ceiling. "It's Saturday! Why do I have to wake up early on Saturday?" she complained.

"We discussed this before! If it was important to your dad, it's important to us, end of story. Now, hurry up!"

After washing her face, Joy gazed at her reflection in the mirror. As she dragged a brush through her slightly curly hair, she took inventory.

Strawberry-blonde hair—okay; green eyes—okay; freckles on nose—YUCK.

Walking at a pace that would earn her last place at a turtle race, Joy appeared at Jennifer's side, dressed in denim shorts and an oversized pink t-shirt. After rubbing her eyes, she frowned.

"What do you want me to do?" she asked, her slouched posture signaling her complete lack of interest and enthusiasm.

"Load these jars with the pink bows in the car. Besides, Rose and the youth group, we have to make an extra stop today."

***

As they inched along Rose's oak-lined driveway, the crackle of crushed rock announced the arrival of a visitor. The bray of a donkey and the booming bark of a Belgian Malinois added to the symphony of sounds. A tiny old woman dressed in purple appeared at the screen door—fretful at first, then smiling when she saw the van park in front of her house.

"Hello, Miss Rose. It's a beautiful day outside," Jennifer announced before walking across the lawn to the front porch to give her a hug.

"How are you, dear? How are y'all doing?" she asked, tears glazing her eyes. "Mark was such a special man. I wish more people could be as kindhearted as he was," she sobbed as she embraced Jennifer.

"Now, now, Miss Rose." Jennifer patted her back, then pulled away to face her. Looking at her, she hoped to age as gracefully. The kindness, empathy, and life experience etched in her seventyish face—the very definition of beautiful.

"Thank you, Miss Rose, for the flowers and for attending the funeral. I know you don't travel much," Jennifer said.

"Y'all are like family to me. Of course I'd go. My own family lives in Georgia, so I don't see them a lot. Speaking of family, how's Miss Joy today?" she shouted.

Smirking, Joy crossed the lawn to deliver the jar of honey with a generous hug.

"Good to see you, Miss Rose," she beamed.

"Sugar plum, if you aren't voted the smartest, prettiest girl in your school, then they're all crazy!" Rose said as she hugged her.

"Tell my Mom that. She still treats me like a baby!" Joy whined.

"You're not grown up or perfect, Joy. Truth is, at this age, you've got the common sense of a newborn fawn. You don't know the difference between the wolf, the goat, the dog, and the foal," Rose said.

"You mean like Dad?" Joy blurted.

"Your dad was a righteous, trusting man who allowed the *wrong* of a situation to blind him to the danger. Obviously, he made a lot of good decisions to live as long and as happily as he did. Another thing, Joy—for the fawn, death is one bad decision away. For your teenage friends and classmates, the same applies—not all of them will live long enough to turn twenty," Rose sermonized with a frown.

"Anything else you want to preach about?" Joy questioned as she folded her arms across her chest and stepped back a few steps.

"Yes, come here and give me another hug. You know your mom and I love you. We want to help you become a big old doe," she giggled.

"Just what I always wanted to be, a big old doe!" Joy laughed as she reveled in the moment.

"Remember, 'Knowledge is power.' Someone smart said that. One last thing, Joy—your dad was a hero. His actions stopped that moron from dropping more lumber onto the road. There's no doubt he saved many lives that day," Rose said, suddenly serious.

"So, my dad is a martyr? He'd save others, but not save himself for his family? Why would complete strangers mean more to him than us? What is—" Joy asked.

"Know this, Joy," Jennifer interrupted. "Your dad would never do that! He didn't imagine he'd be shot, but if it had to happen, he'd be happy that lives were saved in the process. Don't dishonor his memory by ignoring that!"

With a shrug of her shoulders and a roll of her eyes, Joy turned on her heel to walk to the backyard to see Brewster, the dog.

***

"Camille, are you home?" Jennifer called out as she and Joy stood on her front porch, holding a few jars of honey as the sun began its descent for a restful night. A violet-blue sky painted with broad-brushed streaks of sweet potato orange and watermelon pink provided the perfect backdrop for their surprise visit. Grass green curtains danced in the screened windows as country music wafted their way.

"Hey, hi! What a surprise!" Camille greeted them as she unlatched the screen door to let them in. "Please come in! Sit down."

"And who are you?" she asked as she stared at Joy.

"Aside from being a smart teenager, I'm not sure yet," Joy quipped.

"I think I'd add confident to your list of adjectives," Camille said with a smile.

"I'd agree with that," she said, her mouth agape in awe of the high-school-age girl who actually *spoke* to her.

"What do you like to do in your spare time besides deliver honey?" Camille asked with a wink.

"I like tending to the bees. I know them. I even have my own gear to harvest the honey. I like wildlife. Dad taught me to 'admire, protect, and revere it.' I love target shooting, archery, and crossbow. Mom and Dad taught me to aim and be accurate."

"Wow! Do you hunt?" Camille asked, wide-eyed.

"No, I never had any interest. I like to rehab animals and study them," Joy said, unsmiling. She refused to meet Camille's eyes, preferring to look at the floor.

"Well, that's so impressive!" she continued. "Kids at school give you a hard time about that, don't they?"

"How did you know?" Joy asked, amazed.

"I don't know anything about bees, wildlife, or crossbows, but I do know something about being different."

"How are you different?"

"My parents were different. They treated me like I wasn't a priority, wasn't important. You're lucky to have good parents," Camille said as she gazed at Joy and then her mom.

"Who wants a glass of milk and a piece of Red Velvet cake?" Camille asked to change the subject.

"We'd like that, Camille. We'd like that a lot," Jennifer said after glancing at her daughter's sunny smile.

Chapter 6
The Show

Camille awoke to a knock at the front door. "Really? It's 3:00 a.m.! What the hell is so important?" she muttered as she slid out of bed and grabbed a terry cloth robe to cover her nightgown. A quick glance through the peephole revealed Grant swaying from side to side, a bottle dangling from his hand.

"What, Grant? It's 3:00 a.m.," Camille stated with a glare.

"I love you so much. My body loves you so much," he proclaimed.

"Grant, go home. Let's talk tomorrow," she suggested from behind the screen door.

"I want to see you now, be with you now!" he declared. "I'm too drunk to drive now. It'd be dangerous."

"Tell you what. I'll call Gordon or Ben. Who will it be—your dad or your best friend?"

"You don't want me tonight, baby?" Grant cooed.

"Dad or best friend?" she repeated with a frown.

"Best friend, of course. I think my dad is a bbbb . . . ad person. He'd probably hit me first and ask questions later."

"I told you he hurt me. Did you know he tried to rape me?" Camille asked.

"I'm sorry. He's a bad person, yet he's the sheriff *here* in Rain County. That's sick!"

"What are you going to do about it?" she asked, her eyes narrowing.

"What can I do?" He leaned forward to balance on the doorframe.

"You can manage him out of my life. Never leave me alone with him," she said as a poker of hate heated her throat.

"I promise that I'll try," he whispered.

"Since you're drunk and disgusting, I think you should wait on the porch swing so I don't have to clean your puke off my wood floor. I'll call Ben now." When she heard the crunch of gravel and the sudden thud of footsteps on her front porch, Camille froze.

"That won't be necessary. I've been waiting for you, Grant. I'll take you home after you use Camille's bathroom," a voice in the dark croaked, a voice that sliced through the air like a bullfrog's call.

That bastard barges into my home and grins at me as he hauls his drunken son into my house! She sneered as Gordon pushed on the screen door to make a path for himself and his son.

"All right," Camille mouthed with a sigh.

"You stupid kid! I told you to stay away from her! And here you are!" Gordon said as he grabbed his son's neck in a chokehold.

"Where's the bathroom?" he shouted.

"Turn right, first door on the right," Camille answered, shadowing them along the narrow hallway.

"Stop! Stop!" Grant whined.

With an arm wrapped around Grant's waist, Gordon bent his son over the toilet and rammed his finger up into his mouth using his left hand. Camille turned her head to spare herself the memory and to give Grant some dignity.

In an instant, the room filled with the pungent smell of whiskey,

Coke, and hamburger as a waterfall of brown mash splattered on the seat and dripped onto the floor.

"Was it worth it, son?" Gordon asked as Grant continued to retch.

"Nooooo!"

"Clean your face and meet me in the living room!" he ordered, tossing the "for visitors only" hand towel, embroidered with yellow roses, to him. Spinning around to face Camille, he pointed his finger in her face. "Are you too stupid to respect my warning?"

Lowering her eyes, she thought, *Never imagined I'd deal with this sicko when I volunteered to be the teenage outreach coordinator for the police department.*

A bare-chested, red-faced Grant walked into the room.

"All better? Did you clean the vomit out of your hair?" she inquired with a twinge of sarcasm.

"You disappoint me, son," Gordon remarked before his first punch hit home, square into Grant's solar plexus.

"Don't, Dad! Don't!"

"What? You don't want the vagina, the help, to see you like this?" he asked as he landed another punch in Grant's stomach.

"Please stop, Dad!" he cried out as he doubled over.

"I'm kind of enjoying kicking your ass!" Gordon said, smiling and turning toward Camille. Now adjacent to Grant, he karate-kicked him from the side.

Grant tumbled toward the couch with a yelp, like an abused pup.

"No! No more!" he pleaded, cowering.

"Now," he said as he grabbed Camille's arm. "I'm going to enjoy the help's vagina while you watch and wait."

After pinning her arms against the wall, he looked over his shoulder at his son. "Ready for the show?" he shouted with a smirk.

Camille turned her face away, hoping he wouldn't see her deep-rooted revulsion. Her body was red-hot with fury, which must cool like metal to be strong. She willed it be ice cold.

Get it over with! What else can I do?

As Gordon moved closer to her, Grant screamed.

"No! Dad, don't! Don't treat her like Mom!"

"Shut up! She's doing this because she's my bitch. You don't get that. Do you, son?"

"What do you mean?" he asked, tears filling his eyes.

"She wants to please me because she doesn't want to go to jail like her fucked-up family," he mocked.

"Why would she do that?" he sniffled.

"Because I caught her screwing you when she was legally an adult and you were a minor. Remember when I found you two parked off Blueberry Lane at the old barn two months ago? You were fornicating in the backseat when I tapped on the window. An adult, nineteen-year-old Camille, and a minor, you, equals jail time and more shame on her family name. No one would take her word over mine. Besides, the victim wouldn't testify against me," he cackled.

"Enough! It's time, Camille," he croaked as he pressed against her. She bristled as she became aware of the burning urge to shutdown *first* then wage war. *Can't fight sheriff, not this time. He can beat me, rape me, kill me and cover it up. Must check out mentally. Have to go to my happy place and stay there. It may buy me another day, another day to find a way to put him behind prison bars with lusty cop-hating gangsters and felons.*

"No! I won't watch this, and I won't let you do this!" Grant said as he lunged at his dad, tackling him to the floor.

Camille leaped out of the way and waited for an opportunity to grab a lamp to leverage the situation in her favor.

With a single punch, Gordon knocked Grant out cold.

Camille studied the door, weighing her odds, and then dropped to her knees in front of Gordon.

"I didn't invite him here. I didn't want him here," she pleaded. "Please don't hurt me again," she begged.

***

Camille stared at Grant, now handcuffed to the couch. Her face was swollen and bloody, her clothes torn away. Her nakedness revealed an impressionist's depiction of physical abuse, with a colorful display of bruises and welts. She leaned against a chair, shivering and crying.

"Now, begin. Put on a good show for my boy!" Gordon said as he jerked Camille to her feet, shoving her into the wall before pulling a condom from his pocket. The rip of the packet was more cringe-worthy for Camille than the sight of her own battered body. As Gordon moaned and she screamed, Grant cried.

"Be a man, Grant. Don't be a baby! She brought this on herself. It's all her fault. She brings out the bad in you—and me, too. I give you an A so far, Camille. Now, face my son on all fours while I enjoy his girl," Gordon ordered.

Camille cried out as Gordon covered her, and Grant struggled to look away. She tried to avoid looking into Grant's glazed eyes. But when she met his eyes, she could almost see Gordon's luminous smile as she quietly died underneath him.

Chapter 7
Relocation

Camille contemplated suicide as she washed Gordon's sweat, saliva and smell off her body. She winced as she dried her black and blue body. The bruises evidenced the scars on her soul. She breathed as if she'd lost half of her heart and one of her lungs. She'd overcome that, as she had in the past.

She rinsed her mouth with vodka, and then stood in front of the mirror, clad in her chartreuse terry cloth robe. Pulling her hair into a ponytail, she hardly recognized her face, an abstract painting of red, black, and blue. Her eyes, encircled like a raccoon's. Her lip, curled up like a rabid dog's.

"How could trying to do something good lead to so much misery in my life? How did I manage to end up a . . . a battered woman in just two months?" she wondered aloud.

She remembered why she joined the Rain County Outreach Program as a volunteer: to help other kids saddled with bad parents like she was. Learn why her parents chose to disrespect their own lives and hers. Impact teens' lives in a positive, uplifting way because she had walked in their shoes.

"Such a sham!" she said.

Disapproval, a dark demon, threatened to suffocate her as much as the abuse. The engraved pocketknife with a pearl inlaid grip, given to her by her grandmother, called to her from the top bathroom drawer. It always provided the self-imposed punishment when she made mistakes or became disgusted with her life, but today was different—a time for reflection.

"No! He doesn't own me!" Dressing in a billowy blue shirt and shorts, she grabbed her keys and cell phone to go for a drive.

***

Camille paused on Jennifer's porch and breathed deeply to soak in the floral scents, the warmth, and the serenity that her surroundings offered. The sun began to rise from its lair to warm the day. Moments of peace and beauty enveloped her like the lazy spring days she had experienced with her grandmother. In the town park, they tossed bits of bread to the ducks from the pond bridge and gawked at the geraniums and flourishes of bluebonnets.

"Sorry I didn't call, Jennifer. A country drive seemed like a good idea today. I brought peaches that my grandmother canned."

"No problem. Please come in. Please sit a . . . nd stay a while," she coaxed as Camille removed her sunglasses, revealing two black eyes. "Good grief! What happened to you?" she asked, her forlorn expression registering immediate understanding.

"Do you want the short version or the long version?"

"Give me one quick second to check on Joy's whereabouts," Jennifer said as she rushed to the screened back door. "She'll be out there for hours with her archery set and targets," she assessed. When she turned her attention back to Camille, she sat next to her on the couch. "Whatever you feel comfortable with."

"Gordon did this. He raped me in front of his son. He beat him, too, before forcing him to watch," Camille sputtered.

"My heart goes out to you," she said with a hug. The sting of empathy reflected in her wincing eyes.

"What are you going to do? Can I help?" Jennifer offered.

"If you listen and help me sort out my thoughts, I'd be very grateful. I know I need to keep them out of my life, especially Grant. I can't file charges, but I'll cut all ties to them. My motives were pure, but it just made me a naïve target for Grant first and then his dad. Grant began flirting with me from my first day on the job." Camille rubbed her eyebrows as she pieced together the fabric of her folly.

"*Why* can't you file charges?"

"Gordon caught Grant and me having sex. At the time, he was not quite eighteen and I had just turned nineteen, so I could face jail time."

"Tell you what. If it doesn't bother you, we should take pictures of your injuries and keep them on my phone. And you should take another step—move out of that house. Don't be a soft target that lives alone. Surround yourself with people, good people."

"But my home, my grandmother's house!"

"Exactly, find an agent to sell it. Would your grandmother want you to live there and deal with Gordon like you did? If your beloved grandmother—who loved you unconditionally—wouldn't approve, you shouldn't approve, either. Grant simply isn't good enough for you or your life. You raise your standards and keep them high. I say, and she would, too, only the best is good enough for you."

An epiphany, like rays of sunshine, warmed Jennifer's heart. Truth resonated, hung suspended like a shiny bulb on a Christmas tree. The message couldn't be any clearer.

"Maybe you should stay with us for a while. It might be a good distraction for us, having a guest."

"I don't want to bring my problems to your doorstep. You and

Joy..."

"Gordon knows I shoot first and ask questions later. Already shot him once without apology before Joy. After Joy, I wouldn't be so kind. Besides, people are over here all the time from the church, visiting and checking on us. There's not much chance for him to beat anyone."

"I don't know."

"Ask Angie to watch over your house while it's being sold. You know she'd do that for you. We'll go to your house with you later to gather your things. In the meantime, let's go out back and enjoy the day," she suggested as she pushed open the door to let in the outdoor symphony of spring in to lighten their hearts.

***

Joy jumped and fist-pumped the air every time she hit her sand-filled target with an arrow or slingshot. The galley clapped in approval as they lounged in the Adirondack chairs.

"You goofy girl! You start smiling when you load the arrow." Jennifer giggled as another winged stick whizzed through the air to meet the bull's-eye.

"Goofy? I don't look goofy! Camille looks goofy. It's not Halloween!" she snorted.

"Camille was robbed last night by a bad man. He hurt her," Jennifer explained as she studied Camille with eyes that could melt snow.

"Sorry, Camille. I apologize," Joy spoke softly.

"Thank you, Joy," she said with watery eyes. "Hey!" she said, standing up and dusting the moment away. "Why don't you teach me how to shoot an arrow and use that slingshot? Wait! Do you think you're good enough to teach me?"

"I'm certain of it. Are you confident that you'll be a good student?" Joy challenged as she sent another arrow flying.

"Yes, yes I am. It's time for me to go back to school."

***

As they parked in the driveway of Camille's house the next night, Camille noticed the porch light on as it should be, but shadows played in the front curtains, those lights left off. A silhouette of a person paced back and forth behind the curtains.

"I don't want to go in there now," Camille said, trembling.

"We'll both go while you, Joy, wait in the car. Doors locked unless I tell you otherwise. Here's my cell phone. If anything scares you, call Angie." Jennifer reached under the seat, grabbed something, and put it in her purse. As they walked away from the car, Jennifer discreetly handed the object to Camille.

"Wh . . . at?" Camille muttered.

"Put this in your pocket or in your purse. You should keep a Taser with you until the dust settles, especially since you have no skills with firearms."

"Of course, yes," Camille said as she pushed it into her front pocket, hidden by her billowy shirt.

As she inched near the door, she could hear the weather report on the ten o'clock news.

Twisting the doorknob, she gave it a nudge. And that's when she saw Grant pacing the living-room floor.

"How did you get in? I've never bothered to give you a key," Camille asked.

"Look, that's not important now. My dad crossed a line with me last night. We . . ." he stopped midsentence when Camille sidestepped at the entryway to let Jennifer into the room.

"She's leaving tonight. Leaving you and your sick dad in the dust. Understand?" Jennifer snarled.

"Camille, I'll fix this," Grant said, snubbing Jennifer.

"You can't fix him. You can only leave him. He's toxic for you, and you're toxic for me. I quit my job in his office as of now. As for you, you stay away from me," Camille warned.

"The plans you and I had for that program would be life-changing for at-risk kids," Grant reminded her gently as he stepped toward her with open arms.

"At-risk kids don't need the guidance of a violent rapist like your dad! I shudder to think what he'd do to or with a young girl—probably find a way to pimp her. He's a woman-hater, a misogynist." Her eyes blazed as she continued, "I won't seek out and locate those kids for you. It would wreck their lives."

"Please let me make this up to you. One more chance," Grant begged.

"It's hard not to cower around him, isn't it, Grant? You didn't seem to care when I told you he hurt me, but you do when you see it, when he's raping me. No, give me my key and get out of my house! Now!" Camille demanded.

"Come on, Camille. Life will be easier for you if you accept me with all my baggage. Do you really think you can keep him away? Will you press charges or seek a restraining order against the sheriff? Do you want his allies and friends to stalk you? Dad knows a lot of people from all walks of life—drug dealers, other cops, politicians, and attorneys."

With a grin, he continued, "Do you think anyone will really believe you? Everyone thinks you're a rebel, a party girl like your mom. Do you think your word will stand up against his when he claims that you attacked inebriated me and then him in a heroin-induced fit of rage? I won't testify against my dad. I might end up dead. My injuries aren't extensive like yours. You'll look like the instigator. Think about that!"

In a flash, his smile disappeared, replaced by Gordon's stoic face and alligator eyes. As he turned to the door, he slammed the key on the entry table. "Here's your fucking key!"

"Pack a must-have suitcase or two and let's get out of here!" Jennifer demanded, her jaw flexing in fury.

Chapter 8
Skills

"We still need her, Grant. Take flowers and chocolates to her. Put her back into play," Gordon said as he picked up trash in the deserted town park at the beginning of the workday. "What do you think of these geraniums, by the way? They look strong and healthy." With great care, he squatted and dug in the flowerbed to replant a flower apparently uprooted by some scatterbrained kid or loose dog. "You know, you try to add a touch of beauty to this dark earth, and someone destroys it. Why do I try?" he said, gritting his teeth.

"You *love* plants, Dad. You always have," Grant muttered as he squinted his eyes shut and frowned. "Yep, I've heard all of this a thousand times. You love plants, environmental causes, terminally ill kids, and motorcycles. You care about terminally ill kids because they didn't create their problems, like most of the dumbasses in this world," he recited as if repeating lines in a one-act play. He looked into the distance before meeting his dad's gaze.

"You're right, Grant. Maybe I'll organize a trash pick-up day for the town," Gordon said, standing up and admiring his handiwork. "Thank goodness for me and the bees. We make this park pop with all the pretty flowers."

"Yeah, Camille needs to come back one last time. Word is out that some guys are planning a motel-room party two weeks from today, and they want a pretty girl to join them for the night. With a group of guys and an overnight stay, we could earn a quick $1,500. Who knows, maybe she'll 'accidentally' overdose and we'll discover her the next day," he mused as he extracted a paper cup from the thorny grip of a rose bush, crushed it, and tossed it into a trash can.

"I'll try to charm her into forgiving me. That's our only chance to nab her this last time," Grant said as he stared at the ground. "Speaking of forgiveness, Dad, I want to forgive you for last night. An apology would go a long way. And if you apologize to Camille and act contrite, it'd make my job a lot easier," Grant suggested, his voice tightening like an over twisted rope as he spoke.

"These rose bushes have yellow and brown leaves! What caused that? Spider mites?" he said as he pulled away a leaf, examining it carefully. "No, son, I won't apologize to her. She picked her fate by continuing to carry on with you. No, I won't apologize to you either. I raped her for you, your own good. You had to see it so that you'd be repelled by her. 'No guy wants sloppy seconds.' I heard a hockey player say that once," he chuckled. "Hilarious, huh?"

"But Dad, I showed up at her doorstep. She didn't call and invite me over. It was my fault, not hers. I went to her house, drunk and uninvited."

"Well, her punishment was punishment for you, then. Right, son?" Gordon glared at his son.

"Yes, Dad, of course," Grant agreed with a grimace. He glanced at his dad for only a moment before looking at the ground.

"If we're finished here, take care of business. Get the party girl, get her stoned, and get her to the motel for her appointment. Of course, you need to figure out a way to explain it away when she wakes up. Easiest way is to make sure she's an overdose victim," he said as he plucked a brown leaf off a rose. "Of course, then we'll need a new recruit," he added.

Stuffing the leaf in his pocket, Gordon slapped his son on the back. "You're a good kid overall. I know you try for me." After checking his wristwatch, he looked toward the parking lot. "Got to go now. Have to speak at the high school about drugs and runaway risk."

***

Three days had passed since Camille's relocation, but Grant tried to refocus the lens in his direction with roses.

Every day two or more of Grant's friends delivered two roses to Jennifer's doorstep, accompanied by a loving note. The roar of motorcycles announced the arrival of one or more of the pride. And each day, Camille tossed the note and the flowers into the trash.

Acquiring skills topped Camille's priority list going forward. "Let's go outside so you can watch me practice," Camille suggested to Joy.

"Be confident. I know you can do it," Joy reassured as Camille sent the arrow speeding toward the bulls-eye. "A little right, but that's okay. You hit the target. All you need to do is practice outside and inside, in your brain. Try to hit the bulls-eye with the slingshot." As she loaded a small rock for Camille, she continued, "It's a different feel than an arrow, sometimes heavier and sometimes not. The hold is different, too."

Camille focused as bubbles of happiness bounced against her skin. Her nostrils flared as they did when tickled by her favorite drink, fizzy Sprite. The oh-so-reachable goal a challenge, a treat, on par with a slice of cheesecake.

"Thanks for teaching me, Joy. I'll practice every day after I finish my online GED work."

"Next, we practice crossbow. Who knows, maybe I'll teach you to shoot next. Then, maybe, you can help me with the bees, my favorite," Joy said.

"I can't even imagine! I don't know what to say. I'd be thrilled!" Camille grinned.

"Hey, will y'all help me with dinner?" Jennifer shouted.

"Let's go. I'll race you!" Camille taunted.

"I won! I won!" Joy screamed as she reached the back door first.

After settling around the table, the trio joined hands to say a short prayer, then Jennifer passed the mashed potatoes to Camille, who immediately passed them to Joy.

"Camille, you don't have to do that. We consider you family now, not a visitor. This arrangement is working out well for all of us," Jennifer reassured her.

"I don't want to be a bother or a burden. I want you to know I can cook—my grandmother taught me. I'll be happy to help with the cooking and cleaning even after my house is sold or rented. I should earn my keep somehow," Camille offered.

"Not to worry; I know you'll figure out some way to help," Jennifer said.

"I know a way I can pay back Joy," Camille said, in her direction.

"Go on," Jennifer answered.

"I'll teach her to drive the van and eventually my car. In the countryside, it's an easier task than in town," Camille said.

Jennifer risked a peek in Joy's direction. The couldn't-be-bigger smile and wide-eyed twinkle tipped the scales.

"All right, safe and slow," she continued, "We all go together the first couple of times. I'll teach her the basic rules. You can oversee her practice around here and in the school parking lot when she learns the rules."

"I love you, Mom! You're the best ever!" Joy screamed as she scrambled from her tumbling chair and threw herself into her mother's open arms.

"Now, time for bed, Joy. You can check the horses before you go to sleep."

When the door slammed, Jennifer grabbed a cup of coffee for both of them and returned to the table. As she cozied up to her mug, she turned to Camille.

"I think that was a great idea. Now, you need to learn as much as you can from her. Another thing, I don't want those guys buzzing around here. I don't really know them and neither do you," Jennifer said.

"Of course, I'll tell Grant it's over, but I'd like to get to know Ben better. He's ripped, gorgeous, and shy. He reminds me that I still have animal instincts. Gordon hasn't managed to rob me of that."

"You need to know them before you roll with them. Don't lead with your sexuality; that's the easy part. Get to know him—who he is and what he believes in. Get into his brain. You don't need a rebound relationship. End it with Grant and focus on something other than your sex drive," Jennifer advised. "Oh, I have a gift for you. Since you've decided to return to student status with Joy and as a GED candidate, you need a daily reminder of your new role in life," Jennifer said. She grabbed a box wrapped in pink paper from the cupboard and presented it to Camille.

"Really, for me?" Camille asked, wide-eyed.

"Just open it," Jennifer said with a grin.

Camille ripped through the paper, opened the box, and gasped. "Minnie Mouse pajamas. Pink Minnie Mouse pajamas! How did you know I love Minnie Mouse?"

"Your grandmother loved Minnie. She always said that it was

something that you shared a love for, besides her red Corvette." Jennifer smiled. "See the word *Diva* on the top. You need to keep that word in mind all night and all day. I tell Joy not to act like a diva, but you need to act *more* like a diva. Keep looking. There's more!"

"There's a matching pink robe to go with the top and pants. I love it!" Camille cried, holding the robe under the Tiffany lamp.

"There's more," Jennifer coaxed.

Camille set the pajamas aside and searched. "Oh my! What's this?" she muttered as she grabbed the little white box.

Jennifer pretended to zip her lips.

"A gold necklace with a heart charm," Camille murmured.

"It's engraved on one side with the word *Bellator* and the other side, your name."

"Oh, I love it! What is *Bellator*?" Camille asked.

"It's the Lain word for *warrior*, which describes you very well," Jennifer explained as Camille rushed into her arms. "It's a reminder to respect and love the woman that you are," she said, returning the hug. "Now, let's hide all of it so I don't hear Joy whine. If she asks you, just tell her someone gave you a gift."

The door creaked as it opened. Joy entered with a mischievous smile.

"Good night, Mom," she said as she hugged her mom.

"I think I'll call it a day, too," said Jennifer. "Good night, Camille. Sweet dreams," Jennifer said as she stood by her daughter.

"Good night, Camille. Rest up for tomorrow," added Joy. "You'll need everything you've got to keep up with me. You're older, though . . . so maybe I need to cut you some slack. Maybe I should let you win sometimes to allow for your advanced age," Joy cackled as Camille rose from the chair.

"Don't make the effort. It's only a matter of time before I win every competition. Then, I can teach you how to be better," Camille countered before spinning on her heels and gliding out of the room like a ballerina. When she heard Joy's weighty footfalls *squeak t*o a halt, she peeked over her shoulder and listened.

Jennifer grabbed her daughter's arm as she bolted forward.

"What, Mom?"

"Joy, I want you to work more with Camille. Some horse time will help her, too. Your dad always said, 'Horses heal hearts and minds.' Remember how he always quoted Winston Churchill: 'Nothing is better for the inside of a person than the outside of a horse.' Another thing, her marksmanship has to improve. Then I think it's time for her to learn how to shoot."

Chapter 9
Bee Seduced

The next day, while standing in the toasty-warm kitchen, Minnie Mouse clad Camille dialed Grant's number while she sipped a glass of orange juice. She shivered, as if enveloped by a sudden burst of cold on a warm October day, when she heard his phone ring.

"Camille, you finally called me back. I'm so excited! Now you realize how much I love you."

"Hello, Grant. Thanks for the notes and the flowers, but we're finished, finally. No more flowers, Grant. Our relationship ended that night. I've had enough of you! There's no turning back, no recovery."

"But I love you. You're my first and only true love. Yeah, I dated and slept with other girls, but you were always special to me. The first time for both of us was together," Grant cajoled.

"Face it—that flamed out! We're over!" she hissed. "Tell your friends that Jennifer is *not* accepting deliveries from the biker bunch."

"What will she do? Call my dad?" he baited.

"No, but she has every right to defend her castle against trespassers. Do you want to put your friends in the crosshairs?" Camille challenged.

"No, I won't do that to them."

With a *click*, the call ended, bringing a smile to Camille's lips.

***

At school, Joy's eyes followed the second hand on the pie-shaped clock in her classroom. Below the clock, a black board covered with helpful tips for a first read of The *Iliad*. She yawned at the thought. As she squirmed in her seat, time dragged along, seconds like minutes, hours like days. Sunshine beckoned. To corral her instincts, Joy turned away from the window and doodled on a sheet of paper.

"Joy, what's on your mind besides today's lesson?" her teacher snapped.

A chorus of cackles erupted around her like coyotes announcing a kill.

When the laughter died, Joy stood up.

"I get to teach an adult to be powerful today after school," Joy announced with pride.

"All of us are powerful, Joy, in different ways. Some people have to own their power and choose not to. Exactly how are you powerful?"

"Knowledge and skills make me powerful. I own it. I work at it. My parents taught me how to defend myself if anyone ever tried to grab me or hurt me."

"Oh!"

"Are you a good marksman with any weapon, Mrs. Smith?"

"Why, no," she said softly as she glanced at the faces in the room.

"So that makes me more powerful than you in an emergency," Joy reasoned.

"Why, I guess it might," the teacher admitted, suddenly wide-eyed.

It started with a single *clap* growing to a concert of *claps* as Joy resumed her seat and waited for the day to end.

***

"Okay, you're getting a lot better with two of the three tools. Now, it's time to learn about guns. My defense weapon of choice is a shotgun, not a handgun. Unlike a crossbow, you don't have to be the bull's-eye best in an emergency. Like the crossbow, you do things the same way every time—especially with a shotgun, to prevent self-mutilation," Joy explained as Jennifer pointed the pink camo-colored youth gun at the ground to unload it.

"Now, always keep the safety on—never red unless you want dead—and the gun pointed up when you move from place to place." With a deft motion, Joy rested the gun against her shoulder, tethered by the strap, barrel pointed up. Proudly, she marched from the back door to the tree-grove gate like a highly decorated soldier. "See? Safe and simple. Now, you try," Joy requested.

"Wait! My hands are a little sweaty, and I'm really nervous." After wiping her hands on her shorts, she took the gun, careful to point the barrel toward the sky.

"I'm surprised! It's not heavy! A box of honey probably weighs more," she marveled.

"It gets better," Joy said, licking her lips. "Are you right-handed?"

"Yes."

"Now, stand with your feet shoulder-width apart for balance, bend your knees, and hold the gun by putting your left hand on the middle of the hand stock, which is here," Joy said, pointing. "Cradle the hand stock firmly in the middle with the V of your hand. Look at how the space between my thumb and forefinger forms a V," Joy explained as Camille watched, mesmerized.

"Good. Now take your right hand and hold the grip of the gun behind the trigger. Hold it as if you were shaking hands with someone. Remember—a secure yet light handshake," Joy smiled. "You're doing great! Now rotate the gun up while keeping your hands in the same position. Snuggle it into your shoulder. Push it tightly into your shoulder so that it absorbs the kick when you fire," Joy instructed.

"This is easier than I thought, already," Camille squealed with delight.

"Now put it next to your cheek and close your left eye. Think of welding the gun to your cheek. Next, line up the sights by holding it level, and put the bead in the valley between the two cliffs. Although it's not necessary, I like to do it," Joy said with a grin.

"Got it!" Camille shouted.

"Push the safety button so it shows red. That means you're ready to fire," Joy said.

"But it's unloaded."

"Shooting is for another day. You'll practice archery, sling, and crossbow, adding on the gun handling at the end," Jennifer decided.

***

As the sun supervised, Camille yawned and stretched before bounding from bed to bathroom to dress for the day. She smiled at her nearing-normal, mottled reflection in the mirror. She hugged herself, brushed her teeth, dressed in a lemon yellow short set and bolted down the stairs.

"If I remember correctly, today is the day I shoot and learn about bees," she said as she leaned against the kitchen counter, sipping orange juice.

"Since Joy is still asleep, let's check on the bees," Jennifer suggested. "I'll wear my suit, and you wear Mark's, since you're taller than I am." As she shimmied into the suit, she continued, "Our bees are not prone to being aggressive and stinging like the Africanized bees. Those bees are evil—easily angered and extremely aggressive. Anyway, always remember for any one bee sting, many more are likely to occur in rapid succession because bees mark their target with an attack pheromone to lure the rest of the infantry to the fight."

"Ewww! How can I tell the difference?" Camille winced.

"If it's a big hive, that's a clue, but mainly, it's their take-no-prisoners behavior. And don't ever wear perfume around them. It can be a death sentence," Jennifer said, adjusting her bee veil. "Today, we'll get a bird's-eye view of the bees so you can see how they act."

"Did a love of bees bring you and Mark together?" Camille asked as they wandered outdoors.

"Actually, we met through the church youth group, but the bees played a big role in our relationship when we dated and when we married," she said as she slowly checked the hive. "He recruited me to help him deliver gifts of honey to isolated and lonely seniors like Rose. Rose told me that she wanted to curl up and die when Mark passed. He was a lifeline for her and many others like her. It's not just the companionship; it's the idea that someone cares enough to check in, to respect them as vital, wise, and worthy. It gives these folks a goal, to be around for the next delivery. I'm glad Rose has Brewster. He protects her and gives her lonely life purpose," Jennifer explained.

"What a noble cause!" Camille commented, looking off into the distance. "Would it be too personal to ask about the honey and your relationship? How did it play a big role?"

Red-faced, at first, then smirking and looking away with misty eyes, Jennifer wiped away her tears and began.

"At first, when we started dating, he'd reward me for helping him with the hives by kissing my hand. Later on, he'd paint honey in the palm of my hand and lick it off. Eventually, he painted my lips with it before he kissed me," Jennifer said, casting her eyes at the ground to reminisce. "When we married, the honey became very erotic for both of us, since we smeared it on each other's . . . Well, you get the idea," she said as she dabbed her tears with her veil.

"*Wow*! Hot and romantic! I never knew any male that gentle in my life! I never they existed. Elation first, followed by the sad slap of sorrow, guided Camille to an epiphany. "Lowlifes! My first love and boyfriend, a lowlife! What a leech Grant is! And his dad a heartless hypocritical criminal with a badge! He's the grand puppeteer in this town!" Camille shivered as snakes of disgust and fear slithered down her spine.

"Don't ever forget how dangerous Gordon is. Grant has some conscience, but Gordon has the conscience of a brown recluse spider," Jennifer said, her words razor-sharp and exacting.

Camille rubbed the back of her neck and sighed before making a fist to pummel her palm.

"Stop! We can do something constructive with all of that energy," Jennifer interrupted.

"Now, let's go meet the bees."

Chapter 10
Plans Interrupted

Bzzzzz. A small black cloud of bees surrounded Joy and Camille as they stood near the hive. Camille cast a furtive glance at the honeysuckle clinging to the mammoth oak near the horse paddock in the hope they would cluster there.

"What do you think, Camille? They couldn't be cooler!" Joy gushed as she held out her arms, at shoulder level, for the dozens of bees to explore. "It makes you feel bulletproof. 'One with nature,' as Dad would say." Joy added with a smile. "Even if they cover my suit completely, I'm not afraid. I know how to act."

"It's scary, but wonderful," Camille said as she slowly raised her arms to mimic Joy, as a burst of bees hovered around her. "They aren't aggressive. None of them are trying to sting me. Why . . . they hang in the air like hummingbirds."

"Yes, if they land on your mask, they're prone to sitting, not stinging. Bee populations have experienced steady declines over the years. It makes me happy that we can give them a good home. We wouldn't have flowers, fruits, or vegetables without them," Joy explained.

"I like them as much as ladybugs," Camille muttered as she ogled them. "They're whimsical and magical like the fireflies that I played with when I was a kid."

***

As the sun rose higher in the east, three belles stood with arms outstretched to bask in the warmth of the day and in wonder of the bees. Behind them, pastel shirts and purple towels, hanging on a clothesline, danced with the breeze.

"I could stay here forever," Joy squeaked, her voice choking with emotion. "Dad, Mom, and I used to do this all the time."

Camille glanced at Jennifer, now a statue staring at the ground, head tilted down as silence commandeered the moment.

"Hey, girls, isn't this the day I get to shoot?" Camille mentioned with a smile.

"Yes, we'll do that now. Won't we, Mom?" Joy said. "Won't we?" she repeated. Moving to face her motionless mom, she covered Jennifer's hands with her own to gently guide them to her sides. "Let's go, Mom. We're going to be okay, you and me. I just know it," she said, taking Jennifer's hand to lead her back to the house.

"These suits are easy to shimmy into and out of. I never thought they would be comfortable, lightweight, and *protective*," Camille observed as they slipped out of their gear.

"By the way, the lot behind us is vacant, but we like to go to the range to shoot, just to be safe," Joy explained as she began gathering guns and ammo to pack in the van.

Jennifer sat at the kitchen table and wept into her cupped hands, filling them with tears. "I still can't think about him, about us! I shut down!"

As Camille moved to comfort her, Joy shook her head in disapproval.

"All set to go. You going, Mom?" Joy asked. She stood behind her mom's chair and massaged her shoulders.

"I'll drive us if you give me directions, Joy, and—" Camille said as her eyes shifted from Joy's to Jennifer's face.

"Yes, I want to," Jennifer interrupted. After she stood and wiped away the streams of tears with her shirtsleeves, she turned to Camille with a stoic stare. "You'd be surprised at how valuable gun know-how can be."

***

At the range, Camille loaded the shotguns under close supervision by both Jennifer and Joy. They stood under sheet metal roofing, supported by four posts, populated with picnic tables for spectating and equipment placement. Down range, red and black paper targets beckoned as seductive as an anchored sailboat bobbing in the water. The gun range owner, a long-time friend, offered them unrestricted access to move around on the range, an especially easy decision given the lack of customers on site. With an exchange of knowing and wicked smiles, Jennifer and Joy began the lesson.

"Okay, let's stand 40 feet from your target," Joy said as she led the way.

"All right, check the safety again. Get into position, wedging shotgun into shoulder. Aim at the target and take the safety off. Slow squeeze," Jennifer chanted as she pulled the trigger. "Now, if you think of someone you hate, this becomes very easy." Three shots sliced the air in rapid succession.

She handed the gun to Camille. "Reload and follow the same steps every time. It must become habitual and quick. Be sure to rack it between shots. You'll become quick like me with practice."

With the confidence of an Olympic marksman, Camille took the gun, followed the sequence, and fired the shot, obliterating the paper target. Pausing and smiling, she aimed again and fired off three shots. "Yes, thinking of Gordon does make it easier," she crowed.

"Joy, take your turn. I'm hungry," Jennifer urged.

Handling the gun as deftly as if it were a cell phone, Joy reloaded and fired away at the target, smiling between shots. "Fun, exciting, thrilling—all at once. Next, I'll teach you about handguns."

"For another day. How about lunch, Joy?" Jennifer asked.

"How about Sonic?" Joy suggested.

"Let's go!" Camille added.

The car ride to Sonic was quiet again as Camille, Joy, and Jennifer studied the scenery, lost in their thoughts.

"Burger, fries, and a Polynesian Punch Slushie for the two of us. How about you, Camille?" Jennifer asked.

"The same is fine for me. Thanks."

As they waited for their orders to arrive, the rumble of motorcycles broke the silence. Camille watched Grant's motorcycle buddies surround their van, parking on either side. Ben smiled longingly at Camille while Grant approached her passenger window.

"Hi, Camille. Want to go for a ride with me?" Grant cooed.

The slow burn of a flame began to make its way to her brain.

"No! I told you it's over between us! Go away!" she spat.

"Well, Camille, you need to reconsider that decision, baby," Grant said, cutting his eyes at her.

"Why would I do that?" Camille hissed.

"Leave her alone!" Joy screamed.

"I think she made her intentions clear," Jennifer warned.

"My dad claims you have traffic tickets outstanding. He plans to cuff you and put you in jail. I think I can help you with that."

"I don't have any outstanding traffic tickets!"

"Do you want to tell him that? Do you think he'll listen?" Grant challenged.

"Don't go with him, Camille! I'll pay off any tickets!" Jennifer yelled.

"Right," he said, snickering. "That's a good temporary solution—until more tickets appear," Grant advised. "Will you let your friends be dragged down by your problems? Is that any way to pay them back for their good deeds?"

"Get away from my car, Grant! Now!" Jennifer ordered, leveling her Glock at Grant.

"Are you going to shoot the sheriff's son in front of his friends for talking to someone? I don't think so." Turning his attention back to Camille, he continued, "Well, Camille, are you going to let them lay down their lives for you? Think about Dad and all of his friends, allies, and connections—politicians, peace officers, attorneys, addicts, and folks just needing a favor. Tsk, tsk. What a shame if he had to make a call," he said with a shake of his head in mock concern. "Haven't they suffered enough this year?"

"All right! I'll go!" Camille answered, pushing the door open.

Grant extended his hand to help her out. Refusing it, she sprang from the van and slapped his face.

"That's better, Camille. Now, if you'll wait for me by my bike, we'll almost be ready to go," he said before leaning into the cab.

"Jennifer, Jennifer. Don't bring any problems to your front door. Don't invite my dad to your doorstep with bad decisions," he advised. "Tsk, tsk. Too bad, you live there all alone without a husband, just you and your pretty young daughter," he said in false sympathy. "Did you ever wonder why my dad is so powerful? Why the trucks from Mexico pass through this town? I'll tell you why. He has a high-level government connection that helps him, who has his back. Where does this guy work? Is it ATF, DEA, FBI or Department of Justice? Who knows? But I promise you, if someone snitches, he'll know. Kind of scary, huh?"

Jennifer stared straight ahead, gripping the steering wheel and gritting her teeth in fury.

Strutting like a rooster, Grant walked back to his bike.

"Let's ride, my friends," Grant urged like a commanding officer waving his troops onward.

***

The journey to the Best Value Inn, the only motel in town, ended fifteen minutes after it began.

Grant parked his bike in front of the check-in office, leaving Camille standing next to the bike to wait, surrounded by his cronies. Camille shuddered as she considered the possibilities. Dirty-motor-oil dread filled her throat and nostrils as her lungs struggled for air. Her heart hammered at her chest like a drum played by a hyperactive six-year-old.

Are Grant and his friends planning to rape me? Does Grant want to teach me a lesson for rejecting him? Or is Gordon lying in wait to kill me?

She gazed at her surroundings and shivered. The Best Value needed a fresh coat of paint five years ago. The scattered metal garbage cans had regurgitated a portion of their contents around their perimeter. The gutters had separated from their anchored positions. Several shutters hung askew, as if battered by hurricane winds. An algae-infested pool was adorned by floating objects—beer cans, a swimming diaper, and a sprinkle of cigarette butts. Camille doubled over as repulsion and nausea gripped her, the bitter taste of warm lime drenching her mouth.

Daring to gaze at the guys, her thoughts plummeted into a dark abyss. The look of hungry wolves with cornered prey couldn't be more crystal clear. Looking from face to face, she spotted Ben. He blushed when he locked eyes with her and quickly looked away.

Grant strolled toward his bike, whistling a tune while tossing the room key in the air and catching it with the same hand. As a hush settled over the group, Grant stood tall and proud, front and center, like a great orator.

"Thank you all. I owe each of you a huge debt of gratitude that I may never be able to repay. My best friend, Ben, you spotted the van and called the others and me. I don't know that we'd be standing here now if not for you. Since we were small, I've thought of you as the brother I never had." Opening his arms wide as if accepting an embrace, he continued, "It goes without saying that all of you are like a second family to me—a much better family than my first." Looking down at the asphalt for a few moments, he paused. When he redirected his focus to his friends, he smiled.

"Now, if you'll leave, I can handle her from here," he added with a wink as the pack howled in appreciation.

Chapter 11
Grammy

Swallowing the rock in her throat, Camille summoned the strength to stare down her captor as they stood in front of the door labeled number *three*.

"What? If you'd been willing to see me, none of this would have been necessary," Grant scolded.

"Why are we here?" Camille spat, crossing her arms in front of her chest.

"I wanted to talk to you somewhere off Dad's radar. He expects to see us at your house or Jennifer's. This place, this motel room, should give us privacy."

"A library would give us some privacy. This dump probably charges by the hour. Are you hoping to get lucky?" Camille snapped.

"Well, I'd like that, but a few private minutes of your time to talk would mean a lot to me. Doesn't any guy deserve that? I may not have all of the answers, but it's only a few minutes. I promise you that we won't screw unless you tell me verbally that's what you want. Afterwards, I'll take you back to Jennifer's house," he said, meeting her glare.

"Why not talk outside the motel room or at the United Methodist Church?" she asked as a snake of suspicion slithered through the conversation.

"Standing here, in front of the room, makes us more visible to the town folk, which I don't want. We're here now, and the church is just as visible and more of a magnet for people," Grant explained.

"Your customized bike, parked in front of a busy street-side motel, won't alert anyone to the fact that you're here?" Camille questioned as she slid off the bike seat to face him.

"My friends can hide that bike behind the motel in a flash."

"Why would you spend so much money for a *few minutes* with me?"

"I spent a lot more on a week's worth of flowers. I want to end our relationship, if I have to, in a positive way because I love you. Please, Camille, do I have to beg?" he continued. "Okay, I'm begging," he said, pressing his hands together, in prayer pose, in front of his chest.

Camille studied him warily. That's when she saw it.

"That ring . . . Where did you get that cool ring?" she asked. "It's so unique!" She paused before continuing, "Funny, *you* wearing a ring with a cross on it." She gazed at it again. "Now, the emeralds and diamonds I'd expect to see in a ring that you wear, but the cross? Definitely, not your style. Did you discover God, Grant?" she sneered.

The diamond-studded cross ring with four points of emeralds sparkled in the sun, defying description, blinding in its beauty.

"My dad gave this to me. It's a forgive-me gift."

Loathing as scorching as hot lava ballooned in her chest.

"No, I don't want to do this!" Taking a few deep breaths and a few steps backward, she searched his eyes. "Now, be the honorable guy that I know you are and take me to Jennifer's. Be the guy who isn't his evil dad's son, the guy who chose a better path," Camille implored. When he smiled, Camille pivoted toward the parking lot and the bike.

Grabbing her arm, Grant stopped her.

"No, Camille. You don't understand. You and I, we have to do this!" he said, tightening his grip on her arm, pulling her to the motel-room door.

"No, way!" she shrieked. "Fuck you!" After stomping on his instep, she punched him in the crotch.

Doubling over, he managed to stand by grabbing her long hair for support.

"You're not getting away! Give up!" he shouted as he pushed her to the motel, still clenching her hair. "Remember your friends. Think about those traffic tickets."

As they stood in front of the motel-room door, laughter suddenly became audible to Camille.

"There are people on the other side of the door, laughing? What's going on?" she screamed.

"No more arguing!" he yelled as he clamped down on her arm while wrestling with the key.

Suddenly, the door flew open and Grant pushed her inside the room and quickly closed the door behind her.

Camille closed her eyes and gasped for air. A quick peek: a guy in his mid-twenties with a semi-shaved head, and two middle-aged men, all staring at her with somber expressions.

In an instant, she spun on her heel to face the door and grip the knob.

Multiple hands grabbed her from behind while she punched at the air.

"Not so fast, Camille. We went to a lot of trouble to meet you."

"What's this about? What do you want?" she growled, pivoting to face them. "I have an active case of herpes now. Do you want me to share?"

"We're here to help you and help this town," replied a man with a halo of brown hair. He adjusted his glasses on the bridge of his nose.

"You can help me by taking your hands off me!" Camille hissed.

"Please sit and hear us out," he requested as he pulled the chair away from the desk, offering it to her.

"All right. Let's hear it!" she said, folding her arms across her chest and slumping in the chair.

"We're here at Barbara Lockhart's request," Mr. Halo stated.

"That's my grandmother!" she sputtered.

"She contacted our office about a month ago to report suspicious criminal activity in this town. Specifically, she mentioned drug running, theft, and a dishonest sheriff. Does that make sense to you?" Mr. Halo asked as he leaned back against the motel curtain.

Her eyes darted from one face to the next as she considered her reply, fully aware that a wrong answer could easily impact her like a barbell punch to the face.

With a gulp, she answered, "Yes, I believe that's true."

"She indicated that this corruption has been taking place for years," Mr. Halo continued.

"Yes, I agree with her," she said, dabbing at the tears glazing her eyes. "You know she's dead, don't you?"

"Yes, we looked at the death certificate. She fell, hitting her head and breaking her neck. Does that seem questionable to you at all?" Mr. Halo questioned as he spread his arms wide.

"I never . . . thought twice about it," she said as she seized up, tasered by regret.

"Who found her? What details do you know?" he pressed.

"Gordon found her," she said now, coughing.

"Why would Gordon be at your grandmother's house?" Mr. Halo asked.

"His son, Grant, and I were dating. Maybe he thought Grant was at her house with me, since I lived there."

"Does Grant live with his dad, Gordon Griffin?"

"Yes."

"Does Grant keep Gordon informed of his whereabouts?"

"Yes, with very few exceptions, because . . . because he doesn't want to be beaten."

"So where were you and Grant the night before and the morning of her lethal fall?"

"The night before, we went to a dance in a nearby town, and the morning after, he and I were at Ben's poolside cabana behind his house."

"Did you hear him tell his dad about his plans for those twenty-four hours?"

"Yes, yes I did."

"Did he tell his dad the truth about his plans?"

"Yes, he did."

"So why would Gordon be at Barbara's house? Do you have an alarm system?" Mr. Halo continued.

"No, we don't. Grammy always said her shotgun was all the protection she needed."

"How did Ruby feel about Sheriff Griffin in general?"

"She despised him. She called him the Malignant Marshall. She said he was a terminal tumor on this town," Camille said, looking away.

"Why did she hate him so much?" Mr. Twentysomething interjected.

"Gordon's granddad, Jack, killed my great-grandfather in a gunfight in the middle of downtown. They'd fought over property lines for years as neighbors. Grammy said that people do the same thing now, except they use cars to fight for ten feet of asphalt on a public road that they don't even own. She told me comedian Jerry Seinfeld said something similar to that. We shared a love for Jerry's genius," she reminisced. "Anyway, Granddad John wouldn't sell him land, so Jack began cutting fences, poisoning his cows, and poaching on his land."

"What about the town sheriff? Couldn't he help?" Mr. Twentysomething asked.

"No, he was Jack's cousin. He looked the other way."

"What happened when he died?" Mr. Twentysomething questioned, leaning forward.

"My great-grandmother began living her life with the help of a whiskey bottle. She couldn't cope with the injustice of it all. They'd worked for decades to buy that land and build a happy life for themselves and their two young children. She didn't trust any government agency after that. Eventually, she realized that she was a drunk, an unfit mother for her children, so she gave them away to family and friends out of state. Gordon owns their ranch now," she said shaking her head in remorse. "Although other people raised Grammy in Arizona, she chose to move back here to be close to her roots."

"Do you think your seventy-year-old grandmother would be likely to fall?" Mr. Twentysomething pressed.

"No—no, I don't. She wasn't clumsy at all. She was a young seventy, very athletic. Besides, she knows the house well enough to find her way easily in the dark. She was always careful and concerned that a fall could destroy her independence."

"Hmmm . . ." Mr. Halo said, pursing his lips.

"You think Gordon had something to do with Camille's grandmother's death?" Mr. Twentysomething zeroed-in, like a hound dog tracking a lost child.

"Yes, it's possible."

"Did it ever cross your mind?" Mr. Twentysomething asked Camille as Mr. Halo paced the room.

"Well, no. After she died, I became self-destructive and took drugs recreationally. Now, I spend my days doing more positive things without drugs, without the fog, without the stupor."

"So when you decided to make porn films, you performed stoned?" Mr. Twentysomething speculated while searching for the truth in her eyes.

"What are you talking about? I am *not* a porn performer!"

"You don't know . . . You and Grant together, you and various other men when you're unconscious—I've seen it all over the Internet. I've seen the images with subtitles in Spanish. Apparently, they decided to test the market in Mexico first."

"You're insane! You must be wrong! I never knew about or agreed to make porn films!" Camille screamed, now standing and pointing an accusatory finger.

"Unfortunately, I'm right. He pimped you out. Based on your reaction, I'll bet he filmed you with hidden cameras. Would that be possible?" Mr. Twentysomething asked.

"Yes, at . . . at . . . Grammy's house." Camille said, feeling vomit churn in her gut. Her body trembled as the unmistakable truth tore away her protective shield of confidence. With each breath, she felt the stinging, choking sensation of ammonia inhaled. The more she breathed, the more she stressed. Moments filled with silence quieted the room. Camille paced and cried as the truth trampled her self-perception.

"All right," she said with an icy stare. "Tell me how I can help you."

Chapter 12
Ben

"Gather any evidence that demonstrates his lack of character, his lack of ethics. And one last thing, there was a second caller from this location who asked to remain anonymous," Mr. Twentysomething said before he pulled the curtain aside to peek out at the parking lot.

"Okay. Will this other person be helping, too?" Camille queried.

"We're not sure yet," Twentysomething said as he maintained surveillance on the outside perimeter.

"How do we cover the 'party' tonight? Do you have to bust my lip?" Camille asked.

After dropping the curtain, he spun around on his heel to reply. "No, call a friend tonight and ask for a ride. If they ask questions, tell them you don't want to talk about it. If they press you, tell them Grant did something bad, but you weaseled your way out of the mess by telling the guys in the room that you're seventeen years old, making anything they'd do a criminal offense with a minor. Criminal offenses with minors carry harsher prison sentencing. Say that you told them that since you can recognize them, they should allow you to leave unless they plan to commit a second crime by murdering you."

"Wait! Most people wouldn't think that I'd know that," Camille challenged.

"Simple. Tell them your grandmother taught you many things so that you'd be safer in the world."

Looking away for a moment, Camille caught sight of her reflection in the mirror and fought back tears.

"Grammy tried to teach me much more than I cared to learn. She wanted me to learn how to use a shotgun, but I was always too busy for that lesson," she said as her determined mouth suddenly collapsed into a frown. Regret grabbed her by the throat, threatening to suffocate her.

"Look, your grandmother couldn't teach you how to take down a corrupt sheriff, but you can make her and yourself proud by helping us. Now, let's get started!" Mr. Twentysomething said.

As Camille began to dial Jennifer's phone number, Mr. Twentysomething pretended to muss his hair, as a reminder for her to play the disheveled distraught role.

"Jennifer, I'm at the Best Value motel and need a ride." Camille held the phone away from her ear as Jennifer shrieked.

"Yes, I'm okay. No one hurt me. We'll talk more after you pick me up."

As she ended the call, Camille turned to Mr. Twentysomething, the angelic-looking young guy with coal-black hair, dark-blue eyes and athletic body.

"So what's your name, Mr. Twentysomething?" Camille's gaze wandered from his eyes to his lips to his body.

"You can call me Max," he said, shy about being singled out. After glancing around at Mr. Halo, who suddenly decided to cover his mouth, his eyes returned to her.

"What's your story, Cowboy?" Camille asked as she cut her eyes at him. "Let me guess, you played on the baseball team in high school. And, based on your dialect, you're a Southern boy. And . . ."

"Very astute, Camille. Raised on a farm, the land of a thousand jobs. While I learned to think 'outside of the box' and manage my time, I wanted to try something different after graduating from college. I love my job, the chance to do something positive, to work in different settings doing different jobs, and to use my resourcefulness in another challenging, unforgiving environment," Max explained. He smiled, looked away, then met her gaze again, red-faced.

"Where's your wedding ring, *Max*?" Camille questioned.

"I'm not married," Max snickered, still embarrassed.

"Maybe you just haven't met the right girl," she speculated, jabbing her finger into his chest, then letting it fall a few inches before stepping back and batting her eyes at him. "I peg you as a Lazy Lion."

"What does that mean?" he asked.

"You don't have to work for a woman's affections. Girls throw themselves at guys like you who have it all, even if they're shy," she smirked and continued, "By the way, shy makes you sexier."

Mr. Halo cackled, breaking the silence.

Max stared at the floor and shifted his weight from foot to foot.

"Maybe I should call you *catnip* rather than Max," Camille teased.

"I answer to Max *only*," he corrected with a frown. "By the way, I'll arrange another meeting soon. Sorry, I can't give you a number to call in the interim."

***

As dusk shuttered the small town, Jennifer motored toward the motel, hard-pressed to abide by the speed limit.

"Can't we go any faster?" Joy whined.

"No, we don't want to call attention to ourselves," Jennifer replied, fury fixing her face like a mask.

"Listen. When we arrive, we'll park in the back of the parking lot. We'll stay in the car while I call her," Jennifer instructed as she took her pistol from under the seat and placed it in the console between them.

"Now, if any problems arise, the gun can be our best friend against a thief or a bad person," Jennifer advised.

"You mean Grant or Gordon?" Joy muttered.

"Yes, that's exactly who I mean," she hissed. "No one has a right to hurt you or do bad things to you ever."

"Do you think they'll come back for her again?" Joy asked as she chewed on her fingernail.

"Probably, they will."

"What then?"

"We may have to fight World War III. I don't have a plan yet," Jennifer said, gripping the steering wheel more tightly.

Jennifer stared at and beyond the windshield, thinking ahead. "We're here. Remember the plan."

While calling Camille and motioning to Joy to lock her door, Jennifer heard a tap on the window behind her. As she searched Joy's eyes for a clue, her hand reached for her best friend in the console.

Whirling around with gun in hand, she faced a surprised Ben.

"What the hell!" he said as Jennifer lowered her weapon. "What are you doing here?" Ben asked before his jaw dropped.

"If you tell me first, then I'll tell you," Jennifer barked.

Ben began by popping his knuckles.

"Well, we escorted Camille here, which I hated doing. And I worried about her, so I decided to circle back to do some surveillance until I could figure what's going on. Grant doesn't spend money on motels. He doesn't have to. I think it's odd that he'd take her to a motel, then call me an hour later to play poker at his house. Really strange."

"Well, that's very brave and noble of you, Ben." Jennifer smiled as she watched shy Ben blush.

"Thank you, Mrs. Jennifer. Now, why are you here?"

"She called me for a ride home."

Jennifer noticed her answer didn't register with Ben. She watched his eyes soften and a tiny smile emerge as he looked into the distance.

Walking away from the window, Ben approached Camille with his arms outstretched for a hug. In an instant, he submerged his exuberance and waved his hand to greet her.

"Camille, are you okay? Just driving by... when I spotted Jennifer," he sputtered.

"Yes, Ben. I'm okay. A story for another day. What a stroke of luck that you were in the area! Even though you've always been kind, caring, and thoughtful, I have to admit to *hating you* tonight."

"You know, Grant saved my mom's life. Can you imagine seeing your mom floating in a cloud of blood facedown in your backyard pool? Grant spotted her, pulled her from the pool, and administered CPR while ignoring his dad's distinctive siren ringtone over and over again. Do you think he risked being beaten for that? I do. Do you think Gordon would care that he saved someone's life? No. If anyone could weasel out of helping in that situation, it would be Grant. I feel indebted to him. We've known each other since elementary school. He's always been good to me until you showed up on his radar," Ben said. "Besides, I didn't know about Grant's plans, but I was concerned. I knew if I stayed close, I might be able to help you."

As Ben blushed and looked away, she grabbed his hand.

"Come here, Ben. Give me a hug. I need one today." Pulling him into a bear hug, she buried her face in his neck, inhaling his minty aftershave. Grazing her lips against his scratchy skin, she whispered, "Always smoking hot in every way." As he stood stunned, she let her arm drift down his bottom until it rested at his side. "Thank you, bedroom Ben. Uh . . . I mean Ben."

As she walked away from him to leave, he couldn't follow her with his eyes. His libido, lit and glowing, stymied his efforts to be casual.

As she approached the car, Joy jumped into the backseat.

"What was that?" Jennifer pressed.

"Ever since I was small, he's been the one who's made my heart flutter, but his shy, reserved way colored my opinion of him. I thought he was too mild-mannered for me. Some people see him as nonaggressive. Then, Grant and I became closer through my job."

"Ben loves you, Camille. What a stand-up guy! He has it all—looks, brains, and morals. His name should be stronger, maybe Brad. You seem to lose yourself with him. The attraction between you two can't compare to what I've seen of you with Grant."

"When have you witnessed that?"

"I heard about it from kids in the youth group, then I looked online," Jennifer said, shaking her head and shoulders to shrug away the disgusting visuals.

Camille swallowed slowly as the stench of rancid trash—the smell of her rotting soul—filled her nostrils. "I didn't know Grant would do something that depraved. It hurts me beyond description. Grant is officially ousted from my life. Ben is officially on my list."

"How will you handle the fact that they're best friends?"

"That's easy. Before Ben only worried about what *might* happen, when learns what Grant has done to me, I think he'll be livid. Besides, I'll tell him that bullets will fly if forces me to go anywhere again. Is that okay with you?"

"What kind of example would I set if I don't stand up to bullies? A man can't show up on my doorstep and kidnap a family member."

"I worry about you and Joy. I don't want to burden you with my problems."

"What am I supposed to do when she turns seventeen or eighteen? Let him take her at gunpoint because he wants new 'talent' for his films?"

Truth swirled in the cab like a swarm of angry hornets, a showdown imminent.

As the rubber tires gripped the asphalt and the car engine hummed, Jennifer glanced at Camille. "By the way, what happened tonight at that motel?"

"Grant tried to deliver me to a bunch of men, but I foiled his plans," Camille said with a toss of her head.

"How did you do that?"

"I have a new friend, Max. Well, you'd be so proud of me, and so would Grammy. And I promise you, you ain't seen nothin' yet…"

Chapter 13
The Bet

Ben lay in his bed the next day thinking about Camille. Since his dad had held the position of mayor for nearly a decade, Ben knew his own position as a "catch" was secure, but Camille had always owned his heart. He even envisioned what their children would look like. With his sandy-blonde hair, green eyes, and gym body and her black hair, violet eyes, and runner's physique, their babies would be beautiful and intelligent.

Elementary school, middle, and high school snapshots of them together, usually clowning around, dotted his walls.

Their junior-prom picture couldn't be more perfect. She dazzled in a modest blue silk dress while he stood next to her in a black tux accented by a blue silk bow tie with matching silk handkerchief. The gold stage curtains framing the shot added a special touch, the golden couple standing front and center. Of course, the photographer snapped all prom pictures on that stage, but theirs was the standout shot. That night, after driving to a nearby town for a nice dinner, he stood on the front porch gazing into her eyes. Holding her close, he nuzzled her sweet-smelling hair, a mix of gardenia and chamomile. His mom's love of both flowers and oils finally paid off for him as he impressed her with his knowledge of floral scents.

As Camille pushed into him, he gasped as a tsunami of desire threatened to steal his sense of self-control. Stepping back a few steps, he refused to meet her gaze as he shrugged off his pubescent thoughts. When she giggled, he met her radiant smile with one of his own. Taking her hand, he turned it palm side up and kissed the underside of her wrist while searching her eyes, an English lord couldn't have been more suave. Watching romance movies with mom had paid off too. Camille's arm snaked around his waist and pulled him closer. He leaned in for his first kiss, cupping the sides of her face with his hands. A soft, slow, careful kiss sent him barreling over a cliff, sent him smoking and skidding around a curve in his car, sent him fully clothed into a pool on a sweltering hot day. Nothing existed beyond that connection until the lights flickered and an opening door squeaked.

"Camille, time to come in now," her grandmother said. She nodded to Ben and held the front door open for Camille. "Thanks, Ben, for bringing her home safe and on time. By the way, how's your dad?" she added with a smile, leaning against the door to shake his hand.

"He's just Dad, nothing more than that," he answered with a shrug.

"He told me once he wants to be a career politician. He can't do that with a cloud of suspicion hanging over his head. People judge you by the company you keep—like it or not. Can't have friends like Sherriff Gordon. Stories have been swirling for years that a drug lord owns him. Lying, stealing, womanizing, and drugs—all part of his game. People say he steals from the victims at accident scenes. Can't have secrets and skeletons as a public figure. Bad deeds don't go unnoticed. Can't have important secrets and skeletons when dating my Camille, either," she continued, wagging her finger.

"Of course. I'll keep that in mind," he said with a smirk.

***

It was wonderful to date his lifelong crush. It was wonderful until she decided to volunteer during the latter part of the summer before her senior year. His memory returned to that day.

"My parents were on the wrong side of the law so much. I want to understand them better and their bad decisions. Best of all, maybe I can help another teen that's dealing with troubled parents," she told Ben.

"What about working with the youth group at church? I'm sure you'd make a difference."

"No, Ben. I'm not a 'churchy' person. You know about my parents. Everyone in this town knows about my parents. I need to come to terms with their abusive ways, their—"

"But Grant will be there," he interrupted. "He treats women like doormats. He's warped. I'll . . . worry about you."

"You know how I feel about you. There's no reason to worry. I'm a big girl, not a ten-year-old. I've been around bad boys before. My dad . . . not exactly a decorated war vet."

"If he bothers you, you let me know. I'll take it from there," he snarled.

***

At 7:30 am, when sunshine flooded the window of his garage apartment, Ben rose from his bed to check the lock setting on his door. His favorite couples' picture, Camille attached to him for a piggyback ride, captured his attention as he rushed to his desk chair. His growing lust forced him to position the can't-miss picture facedown before opening the middle drawer on the right side of the desk.

With knowing fingers, his hand located the rectangular oak box. Grabbing it, he placed it on top of his closed laptop computer. A gentle touch on the lock mechanism, and dollar bills, razor blades, and white powder appeared, ready to be plucked. His hand trolled the drawer again. Clutching an oblong piece of mirror that winked at the window, he placed it face up on the computer before cracking his neck and rubbing his hands together. With surgical precision, Ben poured some of the white powder onto the mirror and cut it into lines with the razor blade. A dollar bill and two lines of cocaine later, he turned on his computer, raided his stash of protein bars also in the middle drawer, and searched for porn.

***

"How about joining us for a hand of blackjack at my place? How many times do I have to ask to get an answer?" Grant complained as he tossed a card at one of his misfit friends sitting at the poker table in his house. Laughter filled the room when someone dropped their pants to "moon" in response. Grant grinned like a ringmaster at the circus as he lit a cigar, cradled it in his teeth, puffed twice and waited for an answer.

"Okay, after I run a few miles," Ben committed, ending the call. His thoughts retraced the events of the day. *He doesn't know yet. Things are different between us since Sonic. I'll stay close to keep tabs on him to protect my Camille. If he crosses a line, I will, too—to deliver some justice.* After Ben parked his motorcycle on the drive, he paused a moment to gaze at the perfect landscaping—the towering white crepe myrtles, the robust gardenias, and the plum-colored roses.

Yeah, all my senses heightened. The colors more mesmerizing. The breeze more of a welcome caress worth savoring. Coke does that as good as pot, but it also gives me the boost to stay up all night.

Grant met him at the door and invited him in with a handshake and a slap on the back. Walking through the house, Ben noted the home lacked imperfections—no clutter, no random shoes, and no cobwebs. Pushing through the saloon doors to the entertainment room, Ben crinkled his nose as a cloud of gray cigar smoke wafted his way. The cacophony typical of a competitive, testosterone-infused sporting event filled the room. A round table positioned in the center of the room, a deck of cards, a keg of beer—and suddenly, his buddies became a bunch of butt-scratching, shrieking monkeys. At the center of the table, he spotted a can of rose-scented air freshener and a bottle of vodka.

"What are we betting today? Pennies or nickels?" Ben asked as he claimed a place at the table beside four other high school friends—Justin, the stoner with a nose piercing and ear gauges; Aaron, the rebel with geeky glasses and a genius intellect; Joseph, the red-headed jerk rumored to have an undescended testicle; and Blake, the beer-pong champ with one blue eye and one brown eye.

Grant closed the door behind them and opened the curtains to the big bay window that consumed most of the wall looking out onto the drive. Only then did he take a seat at the table.

"Today, I have a pocketful of money, and I feel *lucky*. Everyone else has lost a wad of money to me today so far. How about *you, Ben*? Feel like today is your lucky day?" Grant asked before he tossed back another beer. After four hands—two won and two lost—Grant's smile couldn't be bigger.

"Hey, Superman, how about a big bet. Your bike becomes mine if I win," Grant suggested, leaning back in this chair.

"And if I win, I get . . ." Ben asked as he leaned in and held his hand behind his ear.

"You, you win . . ." He scanned the room for an equally valuable item. "You win my gold ring." He wiggled his fingers like a woman displaying a big diamond engagement ring.

"Well, it'd look a lot better if you bothered to cut and clean the black crap out from under your nails, but I guess we should all be thankful you showered for us today—" Ben said, smiling as he glanced around for affirmation.

"Yet, I always shower before seeing your girl, Camille," Grant interrupted to brag as he beamed.

Grimacing, Ben asked, "And how do I know that's real gold with real diamonds and emeralds?"

"Hey, have it appraised. If it doesn't carry the value of your bike, bring it back to me."

Ben met his gaze, thinking *he probably counts cards, but so do I. Ben's eyes darted left and right in search of a shot glass. No shot glass, no unfair advantage for me. Vodka robs him of any hint of good judgment.* "Okay, I'm in if I deal," Ben decided.

"Done!" Grant shouted as he slammed the deck on the table before sliding it over to Ben.

The cards took on a new life in Ben's hands. The deck mimicked the vertical inhale and exhale of an accordion. They arced and fell like dominoes between his palms and fingers.

"Here's twenty dollars on Grant. I want to road-test that bike when he wins!" Blake shouted.

"Never count Ben out! He's lucky at this game! Remember the nights he walked away from this table with wads of cash?" Justin reminded everyone,

"Besides, his bike probably means more to him than that ring," Aaron analyzed.

Grant paused to absorb those words. While raking his finger across his chin in contemplation, he turned to look at the guy betting on Ben.

"You're right!" he said with a smirk. Rubbing his hands together as if to warm them, he waited for Ben to deal the last hand.

"I'll stand with a King and an Eight," Grant announced.

"I'll take another card," Ben decided, with an Ace showing. "The Queen of Diamonds . . . How lucky for me! Hand it over, Grant."

"Congrats, Ben! Too bad you can't win Camille back in a poker game!" he joked as he wrestled the ring from his finger and handed it to Ben.

"No poker game required. You'll probably do all the work for me by being your dad's puppet," Ben said as he moved his arms and claw-like hands in a robotic mocking way to amuse his friends. He jerked his head right, paused, and jerked it again further to the right like a sparrow on alert.

Joseph and Blake roared with laughter when Ben stopped, pursed his lips, and made kissing sounds at Grant.

"What the fuck does that mean?" Grant raged, hurling a chair across the room.

"I know. Everybody knows. You act like an ass kisser around him. In fact, you have been since we were in elementary school. When will you grow some and be your own man?"

Grant's flying fists answered the question, leaving Ben bleeding on the floor.

"Do you wonder about my pair now?" Grant snarled.

Ben launched himself at Grant like a guided missile. A plume of chips and cards shot into the air as both men ended up on top of the poker table. They steamrolled across the table, exchanging blows until its legs gave way. The scuffle scattered the onlookers throughout the room like an about to explode grenade.

When Grant's cell phone sounded with the ringtone of a siren, it silenced the room. Ben's cocked arm, positioned ready to pummel, froze in place.

Chapter 14
Eyes on the Target

Evidence . . . I dream about evidence. All day, I think about evidence. Must have damning evidence!

Camille awoke with a start and checked the clock in her grandmother's house. She picked the perfect time to be snooping around—8:00 a.m., when everyone begins grinding through the day. She called Ben and asked him to meet her at the house just in case. Skipping her morning routine of makeup and breakfast, she slipped into a green sundress and began the search.

Step one, search the bedrooms to look for surveillance cameras. Hmmm . . . Nothing obvious.

Step two, look for the inconspicuous. Look for something new.

As she walked through the door of her grandmother's bedroom, a grimace pruned her face. She rubbed her neck as she felt the twist of self-loathing tighten around her throat. She straightened the bed and stepped back for a panoramic view. Thoughts of her romps with Grant accented by recreational drug use and alcohol flooded her mind. Disconnected parents, bad decisions, drugs, and alcohol made her a perfect candidate for the role of porn princess.

Scanning the room, she paused to think about what had made her choose to let Grant into her life.

Dad enjoyed porn. He acted like I was a nasty problem when I was a kid. Since my own dad—the first man I ever loved—treated me like I was second-rate, I assumed most guys behaved like swine. When I was fifteen, my dad's eyes lit up every time I walked into the room. I felt powerful. I dressed differently to grab more attention. I yearned for intimacy with a man, even if for only a few moments. I liked being the center of attention, being admired. Ultimately, I chose someone like my dad—lustful and emotionally detached. And here I am—porn princess.

A sudden *creeeeak* startled her out of her reverie.

"Camille, I'm here at your service!" Ben shouted as he walked across the wood floor.

"Thank you for being here for me," Camille said, hugging him. "I never appreciated you as much as I do now."

"How can I help you here?" he asked, returning her hug.

"You may or may not know, but I'm on the Internet. I don't have all the answers about how this happened, but I'm trying to piece the puzzle together," she said as she pulled away from him.

"A lot of people have an Internet presence. So?"

"I don't know how to say this . . . but there are porn videos of me on the Internet. All made without my knowledge or permission. Apparently, Grant hid cameras in my house—he had a key, and taped our sex life for the world to see."

A bonfire of rage took shape on Ben's face as he processed her words. Wincing as if slapped, he closed his eyes, and shook his head. Cradling her hands in his, he looked into her eyes.

"I believe you. I don't judge you for that. Grant's actions reveal his lack of character. I knew for a long time that he was a womanizer. I hoped you wouldn't know that side of him," he continued. "I've been waiting for you to come back to me, Camille. I've been crazy about you since elementary school."

"I was stupid and naïve, but no more. I want to be with you and only you," she said before she kissed him.

Ben cradled her face with his hands as he shared a tingly kiss again with his long-time love.

"Oh, my! I want to stop there. Less is more now. I want to keep this special—do something different—no more indulging the biological urges of a man and a woman . . . For a long while, anyway . . ." Camille said as she separated herself from him.

"So," he said as he gazed into her eyes, "do I need to avenge your honor?" With a loving look, he combed her hair away from her face.

"The ring! Let me see that ring!" After she grabbed his hand, she scrutinized it with a critical eye.

"It's the ring! How did you get this?"

"Grant lost it to me in a poker game," Ben sputtered.

"That's terrific!"

"Why is it terrific?" Ben asked, bewildered.

"Were there other people at this game?"

"Of course—there were about four guys, excluding me and Grant."

"Did they witness him giving you the ring?"

Ben shuffled his feet for a moment and looked at the floor. When he met her eyes, she tilted her head to one side, intrigued to hear his explanation.

"Yes, they noticed—they had to, since we broke a table and beat the crap out of each other."

"Why?"

"I prefer to save that story for a dinner date," he chuckled.

"I believe that's Mark's ring. His wife described it to me."

"Oh, why would Grant have it? I don't—" he stammered.

"Because Gordon, a first responder at the crime scene, took it, and later gave it to Grant."

"Wait! How can you be sure Gordon took it?"

"I saw that ring on Mark's hand the day he died. Now, Grant has it. He told me that Gordon gave it to him. Jennifer said Mark wore it as a wedding ring, never taking it off except around the bees because it causes problems when managing bees."

"I see your point. I think Gordon would take jewelry from a dead victim."

"So, will you promise to hold on to that ring to show it to Jennifer for confirmation?"

"Yes, do you want to take it to her to show her?"

"Let's do it together, so you can witness her reaction."

"Witness?"

"It's illegal to steal, even from the deceased. Gordon needs to finally face punishment for at least one crime committed. It could start a big investigation into what he is and isn't doing."

Quiet for a moment, she continued, "And that would be huge for this town! The tumor finally separated from its food source."

Grabbing his hand, she squeezed it and let it fall.

"Now, please help me look for anything new—anything that doesn't belong in the life of an elderly woman," she asked, glancing up at the corners of the ceiling.

"Tell you what. Search on your cell phone for surveillance equipment," Ben suggested. "Easy-to-hide surveillance equipment," he muttered. "We need to make a 'hit list,' so to speak, and we'll be less likely to overlook anything."

"Smart and hot. Could you be any more attractive?" Camille said as she rewarded him with a peck.

While Camille looked for the equipment, Ben sat on the bed, waiting, basking in the glow of her adoration.

Camille's eyes darted nervously around the room as she viewed picture after picture, page after page.

"At the top of the best-sellers list: a recessed, functioning light bulb; a black USB charger; an Aquafina water bottle; a handheld vanity mirror; and a ball cap. Look for and at hanging coat hooks, black key chains, pens, clocks, a tissue box, and wall air fresheners, too."

"Is that all?"

"No, it isn't. Good grief! Add wall mirrors, clear-lens glasses and the kitchen coffeepot to the search," she said as her eyes scanned the area.

"Wait! Don't touch anything. Put these gloves on first so that we can preserve any incriminating fingerprints." After grabbing a pair for herself, Camille tossed the box to him. "I have to pat myself on the back for thinking ahead and buying these," she said, putting on the gloves.

"Let's grab anything on this list and put it on the couch," Ben suggested. "Well, may I keep some of the equipment as evidence?" he asked with a smirk. "That coffeepot could be a game changer. Besides, Cupcake Camille padding around the kitchen in her pajamas would be enchanting."

"When monkeys fly," she said, punching his arm. Suddenly serious, she said, "I'll keep one or two pieces of equipment at Jennifer's house to substantiate our claims. Hell, maybe I'll keep all of it. I might need it." Scratching her head, she continued, "Let's begin. I'll take my grandmother's room if you rummage through my room."

With data and a plan in place, her grandmother's room took on a life of its own. Hunting for lenses that see, hear, and record every breath. Hunting for lenses that can victimize, vanquish, or vindicate. Technology, once Camille's worst enemy, could now be her best friend.

Chapter 15
Max

Two weeks had passed since Max last saw Camille. Max checked his cell phone calendar twice before including the call to Gordon in his plan for the day. Time to schedule another "party." Before making the call, he called his partner, Jim, from his motel room in Mexico. Leaning against the white oak headboard, he watched the afternoon news. When Jim's phone began to ring, he muted the news and focused on the faded, framed, pastoral picture above the television.

"Jim, my friend, this is Max, the most stealth spy on planet earth. How's it hanging today?"

"Max, the smart-ass. My day wouldn't be complete without your call. What do you want?" Jim grumbled.

"A pleasure as always, Jim. Sunshine can't compare to your warm glow. Anyway, I plan to meet Camille White soon for a big evidence harvest, or so I hope. Do you think it's necessary to meet us at the motel?"

"I have a priority assignment to tackle now, so in a word, *no*," Jim snapped.

"Any words of wisdom as we end our discourse?" Max asked.

"Impulse control. You can become overinvolved and too competitive. Stay safe. I love you, man," Jim said.

"Yes, Jim, I love you, too."

"Impulse control! Overinvolved!" he sniffed.

Opening the top dresser drawer, he grabbed his Glock. His fingers traced every groove before he pointed it at the mirror and smiled. "Enough of this! Time to change!" Grabbing an armful of clothes, he scurried to the bathroom.

After changing, he sat in front of the dresser mirror and studied his appearance, then kicked off his shoes. While staring at the mirror, he pinched his cheeks and colored his lips red before donning the gold high heels with glittery bows. With a cackle, he stood up, tilted his head back, and fluffed his wig before practicing his high-heeled strut. The bra and panties were not a good fit, but his swagger carried the moment.

"Impulse control! You have no idea! I dress like a man in public every week. You say overinvolved; I say committed. You say competitive; I say determined to get the upper hand."

He pivoted on his heel and looked over his shoulder to blow a kiss at his reflection in the mirror.

***

"Hello Gordon, I'm the party guy calling to schedule another date with the dark-haired girl." Max rubbed his leg, now covered by khaki pants. "I assume all of the terms are the same?"

"Why does a young, good-looking guy pay for it? Kind of strange, if you ask my son and me," Gordon pressed.

"Well, my tastes run toward the group party and the rough stuff. Not many women would participate with my friends and me. Of course, I don't want some cop hunting me on a rape charge. I think I run less risk with a solicitation situation. Understand?"

"Errrr . . . Of course."

"Now, are the terms the same?"

"Yes."

"I think we'll roll into town next Friday by five o'clock to eat an early dinner and have a few drinks. Early Friday evening about seven o'clock would be best," Max said.

"I'll take care of the details and plan to collect payment at 6:30 p.m. at the motel. Obviously, she was entertaining. Did you know she likes the rough stuff?" Gordon questioned.

"You mean S&M?"

"That's exactly what I mean. She's an animal—a well-trained animal," Gordon chuckled.

Max felt a grimace grip his face as he listened. When he swallowed the golf ball of disgust wedged in his throat, he croaked, "I'll keep that in mind."

***

Camille and Ben returned to Jennifer's house with some of the surveillance equipment. It rattled from the trunk in kidnapped complaint as the car inched forward along the driveway. Jennifer stood on the steps with Joy, waiting. Mom and daughter wore pastel pink sun hats and waved in unison. Joy grimaced, when the similarity dawned on her, and snatched her hat off of her head, preferring to clench it in her hand. Ben parked the car and popped the trunk. Jennifer, Camille, and Joy grabbed pieces of their stolen stash to carry into the house.

"Do you have a safe, Jennifer?" Camille asked as she scanned the living room.

"You want to put all of it in a safe? Wouldn't it be better to check for footage to lock up? If there is none—only the device—we can put it in the safe, too," Jennifer said.

"If there's no film, maybe, we should install some of the equipment in this house to spy on intruders—" Ben suggested, reaching for his cell phone.

"Good idea, but wouldn't Gordon guess that we'd recycle it when he discovers it's missing?" Camille interjected.

"I wonder what he'll do when he discovers some equipment isn't working," Ben said. "According to what I'm reading, surveillance images stream to a computer. Essentially, there's no film to be locked-up."

"Well, since Camille isn't living there anymore. I don't think that he has any reason to check for images daily, if at all. Besides, the three of us are all under one roof together. There's power in numbers I always say," Jennifer reasoned. "We should use some of the equipment since we know there's no film. It's better than putting that valuable equipment in a vault. It could give us irrefutable leverage if needed."

"I'm sure I can handle the interface with my computer," Ben offered.

"Once again, all of us should use gloves to handle and even install the equipment," Camille recommended.

"Let's store the equipment *least likely to be touched* by people other than Gordon or Grant, for example, a USB plug, a coat hanger, clock or a light bulb. You get the idea," Jennifer said. She continued, "I think I may even purchase a few more items and mark them and add them to the mix."

"That'd allow us to rest easier at night," Camille said with a sigh.

"Okay, let's sort it out and put one recycled gadget in every room," Jennifer decided.

As Camille began sorting, her phone rang.

"Camille, baby. It's Grant. We should meet and talk. I know you want to keep your 'new family' safe. We can arrange that, you and me."

"You know, Grant—family or no family, I don't want a pimp, and I won't be your prostitute."

In an instant, Ben crossed the room to stand next to Camille.

"You've already played that role, baby, unwittingly. Just check the Internet. Protect your family by doing something that is selfless and, well . . . uh . . . routine. I can provide drugs for the pre-evening activities—" Grant offered.

"Shut up, Grant!" Ben shouted into the phone before grabbing it from Camille. "I'll be staying at Jennifer's house to protect the family, including Camille. Camille won't be going anywhere unless I'm by her side. Understand?"

"You'll risk crossing me and my dad for the porn star? What an idiot you are!" Grant chastised.

"Idiot? You want to talk about idiots? I heard every word you said to her. You know, the good stuff about drugs and involvement in porn. Sort of damning, huh? Even for someone with a dictator for a dad," Ben challenged.

"Risky move for you, Ben. For years, for us, it's always been bros before hos."

"Not worried about you or your dad. You'll be viewed as trespassers if you set foot on Jennifer's property. The crosshairs of a rifle—that's a dangerous place to be as an intruder—" Ben warned.

"Tell him I'll blow his head off if I need to," Jennifer screamed as she lunged for the phone.

Ben held up his arm to fend her off until Camille could restrain her.

***

Ben, Camille, Joy, and Jennifer gathered around the big oval kitchen table for a mandatory sunset sit-down.

"Joy, you can go play video games in your room while we discuss boring adult subjects," Jennifer suggested. "Unless, you want to listen to us talk about taxes," she joked.

"Spared! Yes!" Joy squealed as she skipped to her room.

"Jennifer, Camille wants you to examine this ring," Ben said as he removed it from his finger and placed it in her outstretched hand.

She gasped. "This is Mark's ring! How did you get this?" Angling it toward the light, she looked for an inside inscription.

"I was right!" Camille shouted.

"There was an inscription here," Jennifer said, holding up the ring to the overhanging Tiffany lamp to count the scratch marks. Tears filled her eyes as she clasped it close to her chest. "Someone scratched it away. It was beautiful, like the life we created together."

Jennifer shifted her gaze outside toward the vanishing horizon. In an instant, she spun around to face Ben again. After a few blinks, she looked into his eyes. "I must have this! How much?"

Ben scratched his chin in quiet contemplation. After averting his eyes from Camille's be-fair stare, he looked at his fidgety feet.

"How about five hundred dollars? And I'll let you pay it out over time. Does that seem reasonable?"

"You paid nothing for this ring, Ben. You won it in a poker game. It's stolen property," Camille hissed.

"True, but I waged my bike, a big risk, to get this ring, and I physically fought with my friend to seal the deal. This was no easy acquisition," he explained.

"What would your mother want you to do? Don't think about what your dad would tell you," Camille persisted.

"Okay, I agree with you," Ben said, handing over the ring.

A handshake, a seismic smile later, and Mark's ring, wrapped in Scotch tape for sizing, graced Jennifer's left finger.

"By the way, what was the inscription?" Camille asked, leaning in to look.

"'My life is my message'—a quote by Mahatma Gandhi. It was our mantra."

***

At 6:30 a.m. the next day, Camille tiptoed out of the house through the back door. The sometimes-galloping horses seemed to be a little louder than usual this morning, awakening her. Cookie, the palomino Mustang, and Carrots, the big strappy chestnut gelding, usually played after breakfast, but Camille never really understood their silly horse games. She remembered what Jennifer drilled into her brain: *"Horses are flight animals. If you suspect something unusual lurks outdoors, they will confirm it for you. Respect their dialogue."*

Snoring Ben slept on the couch near the front door while Jennifer and Joy slept upstairs. Since school had ended, Jennifer and Joy typically began their day at 9:00 a.m. with a breakfast feast.

Camille softly shut the back door, locking it before turning around to soak in the morning bliss outside. The beehives were still in sleep mode, too, the horses standing statue-still behind a gate and a fringe of trees. After a glance back at the house lights, she climbed through the three-plank wooden fencing to avoid opening the squeaky gate. The sensor lighting switched on to reveal that most of the horses, except the guard horse, faced her and watched her with mild interest. They knew her scent; she wasn't a stranger. The guard horse faced the barn, staring motionless. One or two whinnied at her, hoping for a peppermint or carrot that she usually provided. To keep them busy and pacified, so they wouldn't mug her for treats, she went to the barn to grab some hay to scatter outside. As she leaned over to grab a half bale from the hay stall, she heard footfalls.

Looking over her shoulder, Camille gasped, her fingers forming a fist in front of her lips.

"Love those horses, don't you, Camille?" Grant said as he stepped out of the shadows. "Wouldn't it be horrible for something to happen to them? A 'bad' treat, an open gate, a knife wound, or a stray bullet."

Camille stared at him, her mouth agape, as she processed this unexpected turn of events. She had only planned to scan the outside perimeter of the house for places to put more security equipment.

"You think Ben can protect them, too, every minute of the day? Maybe they'll be the casualty that convinces you that you shouldn't burden this family with your nasty life," Grant said as he moved closer to her.

Camille felt her eyes fill with tears as she envisioned the traumatizing events that Joy and Jennifer might endure—dead horses and relentless retaliation for harboring her. She shook her head, stared at the ground while she... wrestled a wanting-to-emerge smile.

Yes, an alibi to see Max.

Looking him square in the eyes, her steely stare revealed nothing as she announced, "I'll go."

Grant followed beside her as she dropped a trail of hay for the horses to eat. She heard the soft *squeeeak* and *clang* of the farm gate as Grant closed it to walk across the empty lot to his bike. Camille's knees wobbled as she suddenly realized that Max might not be the customer of the day. *After all, Grant had already pimped her out to other men.* As she walked, she plotted. Somebody would be hurt today, but it wouldn't be her. Hatred and disgust filled her mouth like a flood of unexpected vomit. She spat at him before joining him on the bike.

"You missed," Grant chuckled as he steadied the bike. "Camille, you had to know that I'd find a way to win, but you always put up a fight."

He'd planned well, parking his bike a few houses away in front of another heavily wooded lot. After they settled on the bike, Grant dialed his dad. Camille leaned in to listen.

"Mission accomplished, hours ahead of my deadline."

"Good son. I knew I could rely on you. Hey, since she's available now for our customer, call him around eight o'clock to see if he's interested in extra time with her."

Camille watched the houses, trees, and tractors whiz by as they traveled the thirty-minute trek from Jennifer's house to town. When Grant parked his bike in front of the local restaurant, Jimmy's, Camille sat speechless. When she slid off the bike and turned to Grant, she found the question that begged to be asked.

"And we're doing what here? You kidnap me to feed me breakfast?" she hissed.

Grant, who was studying the instrument cluster, smirked as he said, "Always a spitfire. Huh, Camille? I thought we'd start this encounter differently, in a more pleasant way—with breakfast," Grant said as he dismounted and removed his helmet.

"Is it supposed to make my day sunnier because my pimp buys me a meal? Forces me to go into a public place with him wearing my Minnie Mouse pajamas."

"Just play along, Camille. Make it easy for your friends who are putting themselves at risk for you."

Jimmy's restaurant, a standard-bearer for wholesome country cooking in a clean environment, lured customers in with a reputation for offering a gastronomic experience. Tiers of scents, from frying bacon to freshly baked biscuits to the seductive aroma of fresh coffee and deep fried donuts, all available at the soda fountain across from the checkout register, captivated waiting patrons.

Lily, a very pregnant waitress and longtime acquaintance, waddled their way with menus. Short brown, curly hair framed her heart-shaped face. Her doe-brown eyes could warm the coldest of hearts.

"How y'all doing today?" she greeted with a beaming smile.

"It's so good to see you, Grant—and Camille, the one-time tomboy and now a pretty young woman," Lily declared.

With the menus in one hand, Lily managed to hug both of them before leading them to a booth.

Once seated, Lily offered menus while making small talk.

"Grant, Grant. I can't believe how you've grown. Why, I remember when you were a toddler. I'd give you chocolate milkshakes on the house," she said with a wink. "You always had a hug for me when I saw you. I remember one time you crawled out of the booth when your momma turned her back on you to talk to someone, and ran to find me. Bless your heart! You cried when your momma pulled you from my arms," she reminisced before her smile suddenly faded. "Well, I'll give you a few minutes to look over the menu."

"Ordering a milkshake today, Grant, from the pregnant one?" Camille needled.

"Right, a word to the wise, Camille. Lily is one of the kindest, sweetest people I've ever known in my life. If you want to be a comedian at her expense, when we leave, I'll take you to your house and beat you blind," Grant promised, his eyes never leaving the menu.

His tone, completely new to Camille, sent shivers down her spine.

"I think I'm ready to order," he announced, waving to Lily.

Lily waddled back, toting a pad and paper.

"What will it be, y'all?"

"I think I'll have a chocolate milkshake and an order of bacon," he said with a grin.

"I'll have the same," Camille said as she handed the menu to Lily and cast her eyes down at the table. When she heard someone giggle, she readjusted her top to better cover her chest. Silence occupied the space between them as they awaited Lily's return.

Camille looked, with longing, at the bike and the freeway.

Grant's features softened as Lily served his meal. His demeanor warmed as she squeezed his shoulder lightly after serving Camille.

"Now, I have to leave my shift early to take Louie to the doctor, but Shelia will handle my business until I get back," Lily said.

"Wait! I want to say goodbye." Grant slid out of the booth and embraced Lily. "I love you, Miss Lily. Please take your tip with you before you go," he said as he raided his wallet to place two one hundred dollar bills into her hand, closing her fingers around it.

"But, I can't—" Lily resisted.

"Yes, you can. I insist. And I'll be stopping by again soon. Take care of yourself and those babies," Grant said.

As they ate, quiet claimed the third seat at the booth.

Camille sat stupefied as she digested the scene that unfolded, her food merely a prop, a diversion.

The ring of Grant's cell phone startled her away from the graphic, gory array of images that depicted her collection of thoughts and observations about Grant.

"Ahhh . . . Ben. Yes, she's with me." Grant held the phone over the center of the table. "Say something, Camille, loudly so he can hear you."

"I'm okay," Camille shouted into the phone before Grant returned it to his ear.

"Nope, I can't do that," Grant replied. After a pause, he added, "Well, Ben, if you're coming for me, you'd better be packing, because I will be."

Chapter 16
Bulletproof

"Time to go, Camille," Grant said as he counted out his money to pay the bill. As he double-checked his tab, Camille glanced at the expansive floor-to-ceiling window facing the busy thoroughfare that sliced the center of town in half. Grant's custom-painted blue and gold BMW K 1200 S flashed like a neon light wherever he took it. It wouldn't be hard for Ben to spot it parked in front of the restaurant near the front door.

In a single motion, Grant stood up and grabbed Camille's arm tightly. "Looks like you'll be meeting your appointment early today," Grant said as he dialed Max's number. Camille leaned in to hear the conversation.

"I have an emergency. Camille will have to meet you immediately. Is that possible for you? . . . No, you'll be charged the same rate as quoted plus six hundred dollars for the time before the scheduled time. Fair enough? . . . Okay, see you in ten minutes."

After Camille settled onto the back of the bike and wrapped her arms around his waist, Grant let out the throttle and peeled out of the parking lot, leaving a scratch and a puff of tire smoke.

***

Since bikes are faster than cars, the decision became easy for Ben.

Where would he take her? His house—no. He hates being around his dad. He's probably going to the motel or her house. I'm betting the motel.

Ben passed car after car as he neared town. When he finally arrived at the motel, he trolled the parking lot at as slow a speed as his bike would allow. No blue bike to be seen. But while staring at the busy road that led everywhere and nowhere, a flash of blue motorcycle caught his eye. In an instant, Ben sped toward it while his holstered handgun jostled against his chest, almost alive and anticipatory like his beating heart.

After Grant careened around a hairpin turn, he glanced over his shoulder to see Ben in relentless pursuit. On the highway's straightaway, the bikes roared and bounded along the asphalt, jockeying for position. Without Camille in tow, Grant took full advantage of his fast metal machine. Trees, a truck stop, and billboards became blurs of color as the bikes reached top speed. Both bulletproof teens treated the cars separating them like video game challenges to be dealt with a turn and a bit of torque. Horn after horn blasted as they zoomed by eighteen-wheelers, senior citizens traveling to the nearest medical center, and cyclists who had decided to test their road skills with ten-speeds.

Grant made a sharp turnoff onto County Road 419, putting his bike so close to the pavement that only his leather pants saved his knee from debridement. Ben followed, struggling with steering and balance—a bit of wobble, but back on track. He smiled as his bike ripped forward in a cloud of smoke, only a few cars between him and his target. More roadside signs, trees, a few picnic benches, and garbage cans flew by.

Grant must have taken a hit of speed. He's too aggressive and reckless!

Two more cars, an old GMC and a late-model SUV, separated

him from his prey. He slowed his speed as he saw the road wind over a narrow bridge overpass.

Grant tailgated the white SUV plodding along in front of him, at just above the posted speed limit of seventy miles per hour.

Ben imagined what Grant was thinking at this point. *Seventy-one miles per hour! I'm in a hurry! Are you kidding me? Why even bother? Get out of my fucking way if you're not going to push that piece of shit! People drive like they're cruising on a Sunday afternoon! What's wrong with people these days?*

***

Lily bit her lip and checked her rearview mirror nervously. The bike behind her kept pushing her to go faster. "That bike . . . I've seen that bike . . . at the restaurant. That's Grant!" she analyzed.

"I want my toy!" Louie shouted, clawing at the air.

"Give Mommy just a second," Lily said as she patted the floorboard behind her to retrieve the Etch A Sketch. As she swiveled to right her body, Grant *squeaked* in front of the SUV and braked. "I'll teach that idiot driver," he grumbled under his breath. Road debris—an unseen unexpected hazard until he passed the SUV. His bike wobbled and skidded as the tires ran over a large chunk of retread semi-truck tire.

"He's losing his balance with that bike! Can't hurt Grant." Lily's eyes darted to the right for an escape route, but only the guardrail awaited her. The eighteen-wheeler behind her blasted his horn, crystallizing her decision. She veered left, hoping the oncoming traffic would slow for her as she fought with her vehicle. The texting teenage girl driving an F-150 truck with her knees was wide-eyed as she slammed into Lily's car, sending it into a spin and roll. Fearful of the consequences, she pushed the accelerator and sped away.

Within moments, the SUV breached the metal railing, barreling off the road and descending toward the river sixty feet below.

"Oh God! Please save my babies!" Lily screamed as she braced for the impact.

Louie laughed from the backseat. "This is the coolest ride—"

The *crunching squeaking* sound of metal digested by a hard-packed riverbank silenced every voice, every hope of survival. The case of water, sitting on the passenger seat beside Lily, ended her last thought as it ricocheted off her head with the force of a professional baseball player's pitch. A splatter of glass and spray of metal shrapnel reached outward in every direction like an octopus disturbed. The *creak* of a car unstable and unbalanced bellowed out the need to fall again along the riverbank.

Blinking his eyes, Ben slowed his bike to see Grant circle back to the crash site. With a grimace, Grant parked his bike, lifted the seat up and retrieved his protective latex gloves stashed in the toolbox. He slowly put on his gloves, rubbing his hands together to make the latex smooth and tight. Sinking into a crouch, Grant zigzagged down the steep incline to the flat footpath leading to the river. Ben shadowed his every move, determined to help in any way.

The car appeared wadded, crumpled and flimsy like aluminum foil. A few steps away from the visible side of the car, Grant paused, looked away, and passed his hand in front of his face. His look of irritation melted away, replaced by the stoic stare of a paramedic. He remembered his training: eliminate emotions, put on the gloves, assess the scene, and look for valuables. Gordon had taught him this series of steps to follow at age eleven. His best day with his dad ever was the day he got *it* right.

A shriek escaped his lips before he braced against the car to steady himself. He slammed his head into the closed window before opening the door. Tears filled his eyes as he searched for a pulse.

"No pulse! Oh, my God! It's Lily! I killed Lily and her kids! I love her more than my mom! You forced me into this!" he cried. As tears streamed down his face, he glared at Ben.

"Don't, Grant! Please, don't!" Ben warned as Grant reached for his weapon.

"No worries, Ben. I did this. I know that," Grant muttered as he wiped his tears with his sleeve.

Ben lunged, tackling him to the ground. They rolled and wrestled for the gun.

Grant fought with rage uncapped. A back-and-forth of hard-hitting body blows slowed Ben, now pistol-whipped and bleeding. When a desperate knockout punch to Grant's solar plexus stunned momentarily, Ben rolled on top, pinning Grant's wrists.

"Don't do this, Grant! Don't make me hurt you more! We're buds, man. It was an accident. She wouldn't want you to do this!"

Grant squirmed, spat in Ben's face, and twisted his left wrist just enough. Grabbing a handful of dirt, he threw it at Ben's face.

"You son of a bitch!" Ben yelled, rubbing his eyes.

"This bullet meant only for me," Grant said. He aimed at his temple and pulled the trigger.

"Oh God, no!" Ben shrieked as he lay on top of his dead friend and wept. His thoughts ran wild.

He could've killed both of us, but he didn't. He knew he couldn't live with this guilt. I chased him when this happened. I failed to stop him from killing himself. I caused this. I could've called the other guys to help, but I was stupid and didn't. I'm just as guilty as he is. I'll go to prison for this.

Ben cried as he thought about his coked-out, invincible approach to the situation, how Lily would never know her unborn baby, how her baby would never know the satiny feel of a mother's loving arms or the joy of tasting a first Oreo dipped in milk. *There are limits to what I can live with, too.*

As he leveled his gun at his head and asked for forgiveness and accuracy, the shot rang out and his body slumped over that of his friend.

***

"That damned navigation system! It's sending us on the road to nowhere," Sophia growled at Ethan as their blue SUV winded along the country road.

"People at work complain about them, too. Actually, there was a funny news story—"

"Let's just stop and ask someone. I'll get out and ask," she said, patting his hand. "I know that's not your way."

"On this remote winding road, I doubt you'll have that chance," he muttered.

"I saw a news report that country roads are the most dangerous roads. I don't know why people drive so fast, talking on cells and texting. I mean, what's so important? Are they negotiating world peace? I mean, really, is it worth living a life, in a prison of your own making, haunted by the fact that a bad choice to make a cell phone call or send a text ended someone's life?" Sophia questioned.

Ethan adjusted his posture to sit more upright. "It's all about a sense of convenience and the gratifying feeling of multitasking," he said, glancing at his rearview mirror before focusing back on the road.

"I agree, but don't you think part of the problem is that drivers feel entitled and egocentric? I mean, I've seen people in rural areas run stop signs and drive down the center of the country roads to prevent passing. People feel entitled do as they please on *their* road. They feel justified in cutting off or "pushing" people positioned in front of them. That's egocentric—*the world revolves around me*—mentality. I want to eat and drive, I want to put on my makeup and drive, I want to read and drive. There is little regard for sharing the road," Sophia said, throwing her hands up in the air, exasperated.

"Even if self-driven cars become popular and mainstream, there will be a group of people who can't afford to or don't want to own those cars. While the computer-driven cars will reduce the cases of road rage, the can't-or-don't-want-to group will be able to easily tap into the dark, dangerous side of driving."

Ethan sighed before he spoke, "The truth is that we don't know what's going on in the life of the person driving slowly down the road. The driver could be dealing with a family crisis, news of a death, or a sudden illness or identity theft or lack of sleep or a prescription drug reaction; whereas, the person driving too fast could be responding to an urgent call for help from a family member or traveling to the hospital with an injured child. Once again, time to give the benefit of the doubt and share the road."

He checked his side mirror just as the driver of an economy car passed them by, crossing the double-striped centerlines. "I'll be scared to death when Zack begins to drive."

"Zack driving—I suddenly feel ill. Hey, can you believe these mountains? It's really beautiful here. I can understand why Aunt Virginia likes living here. She'll be so happy to see us. It's been a long time," Sophia chirped. When he didn't comment, Sophia turned the radio off.

"Hey, I really need to focus more now. I don't know these roads. Will you look at that overpass bridge up ahead? It's narrow, and what, sixty feet off the ground."

Although their SUV plodded along at fifty miles per hour, Ethan gripped the steering wheel as the truck made the sudden upward ascent. A fear of heights always a problem, even in a vehicle.

"What the hell is that?" Sophia screamed.

"Kind of busy now."

"Someone ran through the guardrail," she assessed as she followed the trajectory over the side of the bridge, ". . . and there, right there, is a smashed car and two people lying outside the car on the ground, stacked like . . . war casualties on a battlefield. How horrific! You—you have to pull over so we can help them."

Wiping his brow, Ethan followed the road until he spotted the bikes. Parking behind them, he turned on his flashers and looked both ways before exiting. A quick check for cell phone coverage revealed two bars.

"I'm calling 911."

Sophia threw caution to the wind and bolted out of the car to move down the steep incline. The hiss of scattering gravel forced her to slow her pace as she started to skid.

"For the love of God, Sophia, slow down! Don't end up with an injury because you want to race down the hill. Ice the aggressive attitude for now!" Ethan shouted as he rubbed the back of his neck. "Thank God we didn't travel with Zack this time!" he fumed, red-faced, as he shadowed her path.

Chapter 17
Collateral Damage

Camille stood at the window, pulled the drape aside, and stared into the distance. "This time it was different—even worse than last time. Even though I knew I'd be safe with you, he was more emotional—more intense, angrier, and very desperate. Maybe he was using, today."

"They want you dead, Camille. Grant told me you like to be rough in the bedroom. In fact, he basically indicated the rougher, the better," Max said.

"And that should surprise me? I'm a witness and an unwilling participant in their operations. If they lose me to an encounter gone too far, you've taken care of their problem. Otherwise, they may have to kill me—but Grant wouldn't do it," Camille analyzed.

"Why?"

"Because in spite of what you may think, he has a soul. His conscience is always under assault by his dad, but he manages to maintain a shred of goodness," Camille defended.

"Why, in God's name, did you spend time with him? How did all of that happen? Don't you feel like you deserve better company? A better guy? One who won't drug you, encourage you to do drugs, or pimp you out? *What were you thinking?*" Max questioned.

"Look, Max, it began innocently enough. I wanted to work with at-risk kids, to volunteer if necessary, and the Gordon–Grant team manages the group for the school. It would've been impossible to avoid Grant—"

"But you didn't have to become involved with him. Didn't you read the warning signs?"

"You know, it's real easy to sit in judgment of me when you don't know all of the facts."

"Well, why don't you tell me?" he mocked. "Let me guess, Dad didn't treat you like he cherished you."

In a blink, Camille raised her arm to slap Max, but he caught it midswing. In a flash, she stomped his instep and attempted to head-butt him and punch him in the face before he grabbed her other arm.

"Your problem is that you need to fight as ferociously for yourself as you fight me. You need to feel worthy of respect, worthy of love. You don't realize how powerful and pretty you are."

As tears of fury spilled onto her cheeks, she sputtered, "The dad who raised me received me as a two-year-old rehomed Romanian girl—a trade for a drug debt owed. There's no oversight, no children's protective services for rehomed orphans in the US. As my Grammy said, adoptive parents can get in over their heads—a kid may have unknown problems or can't bond, and so desperate parents give the kids away, even advertise them on craigslist. The kids are the invisibly visible on paper."

"Grammy said that my fate could've been worse with a pedophile," continued Camille, cringing, "but she didn't know that my dad craved my attention and affections as a teenager. She always said she loved me and would watch out for me," she said as she continued to weep. "She even gave me a knife to protect myself in case I ever needed it when away from home. She loved me unconditionally. I guess I was lucky to have her in my life; some people never know that feeling. My mom, a user, committed suicide by running into oncoming traffic on the freeway. I didn't ask for this home life, but it's all I've known. In answer to your question, yes, my dad treated me like he cherished me, but only for my womanly affections. I guess when your dad treats you like a sex object . . . it doesn't seem wrong or odd when other men do; it's just the way they are. I thought that until I met Mark. I didn't know men like him existed."

Max released his hold and hugged her.

"Hey, I'm sorry. I can be an ass, as I've proven once again," he said with a soft smile. "With formal training, I think you may come close to being as good as I am." Max winked and coiled up in a karate-fighting pose.

"Humor—I like humor. There can never be too much funny in my life," she sniffled, rolling her eyes. "I think we should go back to Jennifer's house before she wakes up and begins searching for me. I don't have a cell and can't call her, but I know she'll start looking soon with a shotgun in tow."

"I'll drop you off a few houses away, so I don't blow my cover," Max said as he opened the motel room door. Head tilted down, he furtively looked from side to side—a fox on the prowl not more stealth.

"Shouldn't we act normal?" Camille asked.

"That wouldn't make sense under scrutiny. For now, I'll grab your arm as if I'm forcing you along with me to the car. Resist enough to be convincing until we settle into the car."

While Camille slowed her pace, she found it difficult to feign resistance.

It's always all or nothing with me. Moderation doesn't fit into my world or my mind.

Thoughts of Gordon suddenly flooded her mind, streaming hatred into her blood supply. She elbowed hard with her captured arm and ducked her head to avoid being tethered by her hair. In spite of the deep lunge forward, Max managed to grab her.

"Good—you have some skills, some strong natural instincts. Mine prevail only because of years of training. Most people, including Gordon, don't have the lightning-quick reactions that I do. You'd do well to remember that."

After "coercing" her into his car, Max started the engine and began to plot.

"Here's my phone. Call Jennifer. Tell her you're safe and on your way back home."

"Yeah, I have to do that so she doesn't blow someone to bits," Camille said as she dialed.

"Damn! She isn't answering," she grimaced.

"Why wouldn't she answer?" Max questioned.

"She could be in the bathroom, or she could be in a dead cell zone."

"Why do you think Gordon is indestructible? What do you know about his operations?"

"Since Gordon is the sheriff here, he has the credibility, the radar, and the perfect cover to find and pimp kids, funnel drugs to them, or make them mules who transport drugs. Grant claims that his dad knows important people to cover his tracks if and when needed. While you can infiltrate his operation, I know what to target and when, his modus operandi."

"And how would you describe that?" he questioned.

"*Eat or be eaten* sort of sums up his moral code."

***

Gordon squatted in his flower garden to snatch away the few emerging weeds. Bees darted from blossom to blossom, gathering a daily ration from the delectable selections—the blue beach-umbrella shaped Siberian squill, the orange sunburst of California poppy, the delicate daisy-like purple coneflower—chosen especially for them. His nearby radio and police scanner sat side by side on an outdoor table. The mesmerizing sounds of rock classics filled the air. The police scanner buzzed and hissed as Ozzy Osbourne sang "Crazy Train."

As a finishing touch, Gordon smiled and clipped the wilted roses off the bushes before cutting a few full blooms for the house. The day seemed special—a day that a death might be reported, one that he hoped for, even dreamed about. Savoring the thought, he closed his eyes to inhale the scent of a red rose and bask in the sunshine of the day, then, he sashayed into the house.

***

Dread congealed in Sophia's throat like dirty motor oil as she approached the bodies of the two guys. The taste in her mouth became both bitter and habanero hot.

Must see if, by some miracle, they are alive. Must be strong and stow emotions.

The wide-eyed, bloody mask of a face stared at her as she put her fingers on the left wrist dangling near the ground. Just as she expected—no pulse, no wedding ring, no chance to enjoy the fruits of a life well-lived. A deep breath hitched in her throat. Turning away, she closed her eyes to take a moment when she felt Ethan fold her into his arms. She inhaled his orangey pine cologne, thankful for his presence, as she leaned into him for balance.

"I can take over from here. It may be easier for me to sort through this scene. I'll check the other guy while you gather your strength. Is standing alone possible at this point?" he asked as hugged her tightly.

"No, go ahead. I wonder if these guys are solid citizens or evil convicts. Since they are both bleeding from the head, maybe they unintentionally witnessed something."

Ethan's eyes scanned the second body before checking for a pulse. A frown and a quick shake of his head answered any question about a heartbeat. "I need to look closer at these bodies from a different vantage point," he said, inching around to the other side. He stood still before stepping back a few times.

After a few moments, he grimaced and observed, "Unless this is a staged crime scene, they committed suicide. Connecting the dots here, the right hand holding the gun is bloody . . ."

He squatted to get a closer look. "And the entry wound here at the temple indicates a suicide or a professional hit. It's bizarre, but the guy closest to the ground seems to be smiling, purely content. Now, the other guy, on top of the heap, is holding a gun in his bloody right hand and seems frightened. Anyway all of this is my best guess as an avid fan of *Forensic Files*, the tv show that you hate to watch."

As he turned away, he coughed several times. "That's all I've got."

Sophia held her breath and balled up her hands as she dared to look in the car.

"Oh, my God!" she yelped as she hung on the door for support. The copper-penny taste of blood coated her tongue as she peered inside the car again. She shook her head and blinked her eyes to reboot her brain as a pool of saliva welled on her soft palate, which reminded her of a stroll by the meat department in the grocery store just yesterday.

A woman's blood-drenched body hunched to the right over the steering wheel, her blue floral shirt now crime-scene red. Blood splatter appeared on the spiderwebbed driver's side windshield. A section of hair hung from a hole in the web design. Sophia looked away and looked back at the limp body, then reached in to touch the driver's neck for some sign of a pulse. When the body shifted, the blood-soaked head moved to reveal a crown of jagged glass. Part of the woman's scalp dangled on the right side of her face like a wig comically misplaced for laughs. Sophia blinked to re-boot her brain before she risked another look.

Sophia glanced at the victim's face for signs of breath when she saw it—the woman's teeth embedded in the steering wheel. Sophia swayed as she felt the hard fist of nausea punch her in the gut. The steely scent of blood and fecal matter knocked her to her knees, and she began to retch.

"Sophia, I'll handle this." Ethan said as he approached the car.

"Oh, no, this is horrific! She was pregnant, very pregnant!" Sophia screamed. "You have to check her pulse to see if she may still be alive. If she's not alive, that baby is not likely to be alive. The air bag probably inflated after the collision. Be sure to steady her body so that half of her scalp doesn't rip away." Sophia cried as she spewed again. "I can't stop crying. My stomach won't stop heaving."

"No pulse," Ethan whispered. He turned away from the door and rubbed his eyes.

Sophia heard deep breaths as she righted herself. Shaking her head and body first, she stepped to the door again. This time, she looked toward the backseat. She felt the surge of hot blood seep from her heart to her feet. A motionless . . . blond, curly-headed, three-year-old boy slumped, partially visible, behind the front seat console. His head dripped blood onto the Etch A Sketch on the floor. A single gurgling, raspy breath escaped his lips. The front seat console crushed him as the backseat welded to the front seat space. After a dash to the front passenger door, she climbed in through the window.

"Hey, honey, listen to me. It'll all be okay. Just stay with me. Now, I'm going to sit here with you . . . and hold your hand," she stammered. The tightly clenched fist, bearing a Marks-A-Lot-made orange sun, helped him anchor his fight for his next gulp of air. As she lowered her head to better see him, she heard a soft, wet wheezing breath, and his little fingers relaxed in her hand.

She pushed away from the car door, enraged.

"Some fucking idiot caused this, and why? What was so important?" Sophia wept, her eyes filled with fury. "I bet one or both of the fucking idiots lie in that pile," she hissed as she pointed toward the pile of young men.

The lifeless bodies of the two friends were stacked, crisscrossed, like random sticks of wood gathered and ready for a match.

Chapter 18
Detectives

At 7:00 a.m., Jennifer awoke with a start in her bedroom. Looking out from the French doors, she could see horses nibbling at the mounds of hay on the ground. When she opened her doors and stepped on to the raised terrace, she paused to listen. Before she returned to her room, she looked at the guard horse, Trooper, who munched hay while he faced the back gate.

Probably another deer trying to pirate their pasture.

Although minor, her suspicions led her to Camille's door. With a quiet turn of the doorknob, she hoped to have her answer. Camille seemed to be sleeping with her back to the door. Cradling the edge with one hand and pulling the knob with the other, Jennifer closed the door and walked a few more steps to the room of her daughter, the other equine addict in residence. With the face of an angel haloed in strawberry-blonde hair, Joy slept peacefully as usual on her left side, facing the door.

Joy snores loud enough to drown out any alarm, Jennifer snickered as she closed the door. *As long as they are both safe and sound, all is well.*

After she walked back to her room and settled back into bed, she rested with her fingers laced behind her head. Her thoughts wandered to Mark and the sweetness of their lives together. She cringed as she thought of her life before Mark, when a cheerleader's worry about a Friday-night football game performance trumped most other concerns. She shuddered as she thought about her misguided attraction to bad boys—boys like Gordon.

***

As the motorcycle growled to a start, Jennifer scrambled to the window to see Grant's bike screech away, with Camille in tow, from the lot behind the house.

"What the hell!" Jennifer screamed as she dialed Gordon's number and quickly ended the call after one ring. A mad dash to Joy's room left Jennifer breathless.

"Joy, we have to go! Grant took Camille! Get dressed and meet me in the van."

As they sped down the road toward the motel, Jennifer plotted to follow Grant and put him in her gun sights to scare him.

"Look, we're going to play detective today. How about it?" Jennifer said.

"Yes! Count me in!"

***

The minivan circled the Best Value Inn once. The horseshoe shape made hunting Grant's bike much easier. The check-in office across from the filthy pool suited Hank's busybody mentality. After all, how many options are there for entertainment in a small town? How many people had as much opportunity as Hank to watch affairs among the local folk take root and flourish?

"Why doesn't he do something about that nasty pool? The entire operation needs an overhaul. I bet bedbugs and lice live in those rooms. One day, he'll probably hang a neon sign with an hourly rate listed," Jennifer joked.

"Why is an hourly rate funny?" Joy asked.

"I'll explain it to you when you're older, Joy," Jennifer said as she continued to search. "I don't see his bike. It's likely that he's already been here."

"Now, what?" Joy whined.

A quick glance at the rearview mirror revealed an impatient, petulant teenager who could easily make this project twice as trying. "Why don't you wait a second in the car for me while I ask Hank about Grant? I'll run in and out; then, maybe we can piece the puzzle together."

"Okay, but you know me. I'm not very patient and I like a lot of sleep, which didn't happen last night. Thank you very little," Joy said as she pursed her lips into a pout.

After she parked the van at the front office, Jennifer noticed a softness in Hank's eyes. Entering the office, the smell of dust and mildew hit her like a slap on the face. Wrinkling her nose, she smiled.

"Hello, Mr. Hank. How are you today?"

"Well, the week got off to a rough start when my office toilet overflowed. I had to mop up with bed sheets when I ran out of towels. Cleaning is not my favorite job. That's why I hire it out a couple of times a month."

He returned the smile, his yellow teeth framed by black lines, reflecting his cavalier attitude about cleanliness.

"Have any gossip for me, Mrs. Jennifer? I'm always on the prowl for good gossip. People call me Mr. Know-It-All cuz I know a lot about everybody's business," he crowed.

"Nothing today, Mr. Hank. Speaking of being on the prowl, I wonder if you've seen Grant today, or Miss Camille, or maybe Ben.

Did they zoom by on a bike or stop by a room?" she said, gazing over her shoulder toward the parking lot.

"Well, let's see," he said as he scratched his unshaven chin and lowered his eyes to Jennifer's bosom. "Matter of fact," he said to her breasts, "I saw them this morning—they drove in and stopped by number 3. Ben cruised through a short time after they left."

"What time?"

"Oh . . ." now his gaze shifted to her midriff, "about twenty minutes before you showed up."

Licking his lips, he added, "If there's any other thing I can help you with, Mrs. Jennifer, let me know. I imagine it's tough for a pretty young widow like you to adjust."

She shuddered at the thought, then quickly recovered with a smile. "Thanks, Hank. It pains me to think about my former life." Shifting her gaze to the floor, she said, "I'll always love Mark." Her eyes narrowed, and she returned his stare. "Well, Joy is waiting on me. Better go!"

"Another day, Mrs. Jennifer, when you leave the kid at home," he suggested with a wink.

As she turned to walk away, she felt his eyes follow her. She rolled her eyes, wincing at the thought.

After opening the car door, Jennifer said, "He stopped by number 3. We'll breeze by and knock on the door."

Another peek at the rearview mirror confirmed her suspicions—Joy's fidgetiness now full-blown frustration. Jennifer sighed as the car crawled past door after door. Finally, she parked.

"Okay, you wait here. I'll check. Be back in a minute," she said before sprinting to number 3. After knocking and then pounding with her first, she returned to the car feeling chagrined.

"Okay, Mom, where to now?"

Jennifer bit her bottom lip while she contemplated an answer to

Joy's question. To appease Joy's need to move along, she eased the car closer to the check-in office.

"Let's sit here for a minute while I think," she replied as she watched Hank grin, grab his cell phone, and push a button.

When he talked, he slapped the counter with his hand as his head rolled back in unbridled laughter. But when he noticed Jennifer's stare, Hank's amusement faded away, replaced by a mouth knotted in a hard line and a steely glare.

***

Gordon slammed down the phone. *The situation with that girl is suddenly too complicated—too many people involved.* As he began loading his truck with guns, he heard the police scanner broadcast a message: "Accident on CR 419 with multiple fatalities."

Could I be so lucky? Could it be Camille and her customer, or maybe Jennifer?

Strapping on his shoulder holster and belt, he paused to savor the moment and smiled.

Think I'll take 419 to town to troll and check out the accident on the way. Maybe there's something golden and sparkly for the taking.

***

"There are three places to check: back home, in case she's with Max, Gordon's for a risky face-to-face, or Ben's to keep us out of the fray," Jennifer said.

"Since I'm not a baby, do you mind moving your weapons to the backseat so that I can sit in the front with you? You can cover them there, too. I'll even share space in the front seat with a few of your favorites. Honestly, it seems like I'd be better off sitting close to an arsenal if I need to grab something. And it would be safer for me to sit close by you so you can be Nancy the Nazi," Joy whined.

"Okay, deal," Jennifer acquiesced as she pulled over to the side of the road and plucked a few pieces to keep close at hand.

In a flash, Joy vaulted into the front passenger seat. Her eyes twinkled as she raided the stash before buckling her seatbelt.

"What is *this*?" Joy asked as she reached for the cell phone cover. "Why is *this* with the weapons? Don't you already have a cover?"

"Good question—that cell phone cover is a tool for defense. It's called a Yellow Jacket, and it's an iPhone case with a stun gun."

"Awesome! Let me switch the covers for you," she pleaded.

"No playing—be careful, just like with the shotguns. I charged the stun gun already. I saved the case changeover for you. Read the directions first."

"Hooray! I can handle this!" Joy said, tearing into the packaging. "How long does it hold a charge?"

"I called about that. It holds a charge for a couple of days," she smiled, lost for a moment in her daughter's sheer elation.

"Done! So cool!" Joy said as she studied the gadget before reaching for another.

"Lipstick? Why would this—" Joy asked as she popped off the cap.

"Be careful! It's a clever disguise for red-pepper spray, effective for up to thirty minutes. It can be fired at a range of up to fifteen feet. Impressive, huh?"

"I wanted a tube, anyway. You should give this one to me!" Joy announced, her chin tilted upward in smug satisfaction.

"The girl who owns a shotgun and a professional-grade crossbow wants my lipstick pepper spray, too. That's funny! I'd bet you'll want everything I brought today," Jennifer grinned.

"And I shouldn't have it because . . . ?" Joy persisted.

Exasperated by the looming promise of more pushback, Jennifer made a quick decision. "We'll go to Ben's. Correction: I'll go to Ben's to see Bruce and you'll go visit Rose."

"That makes zero sense! I should go with you! Ben's out looking for Camille, not sitting at home," Joy complained.

That's exactly why I should go there—to regroup and enlist Ben's dad to help us find them."

"Jeez . . . she's probably with Max, Mom."

"Not if Ben caught up with them before they reached the motel, and not if she's being forced to see someone else," Jennifer theorized with a frown. "In fact, Ben doesn't know about Max. He'd try to fight with him for her."

As Jennifer executed a quick turn to Rose's house, a fleeting thought crossed her mind.

I'll update Bruce. Bruce and I should confront Gordon with guns in hand . . . to get some answers.

Chapter 19
Jennifer's Day

Jennifer stood on the porch, taking a moment before grabbing the copper knocker adorned with the family crest. She shifted her weight from foot to foot while she waited. Early afternoon began to simmer quickly on this hot summer day. She felt an electrifying rush of adrenaline as she rehearsed her speech again.

Bruce appeared at the door shirtless, with a frosty beer mug in hand. "May I help you, Jennifer?"

His too-warm smile indicated that he'd like to help himself to her. His overpowering aftershave made her cough.

"Actually, I'm concerned about Ben and Camille. Camille disappeared early this morning, probably forced. Ben left the house to find her. I need help searching for them."

"Forced? Are you sure? Ben actions don't surprise me. Ben still believes in chivalry. That kid usually acts so level-headed," he said, shaking his head in disapproval. "In this small town, everybody knows everybody else's business. Someone should have spotted something."

"True, but I don't have time to knock on every door. I've already checked one place. By the way, I know Camille wouldn't go with Grant unless he forced her," Jennifer countered.

"And you want me to drive the main drag with you to talk to the business owners? Do you think my position as mayor will help us?" Bruce asked with an arched brow.

"Actually, I think we may get more valuable answers and insights from Gordon," Jennifer said before crinkling her noise in disdain.

"What do you have in mind—a phone call or a house call?" Bruce asked.

"I know a house call would be more convincing," Jennifer said without hesitation.

"You think facing off with Gordon is a good idea?" Bruce asked, wide-eyed. "That guy is . . . well, known to be ruthless."

"Camille is like a second daughter to me. I need to revisit that point with him. And I worry about Ben tangling with Grant. After all, Gordon did shape his son's values and ethics," Jennifer said with a frown.

Quiet for a moment, Bruce avoided her glare, staring instead at the rug on the floor.

"Well, you do what you think is right—just don't get in my way," she snapped.

When he met her determined eyes, he relented. "Okay, give me a minute to put on a shirt and grab a gun before we go. Make yourself comfortable."

Sitting on the sofa, she glanced around in hopes of learning more about Bruce. An easel sat in the corner of the living room, a feminine figure taking shape in red and blue on the canvas. A white leather loveseat and matching couch faced the TV set. Abstract paintings dotted the walls. A dusty bible and a well-worn *Sports Illustrated* swimsuit issue awaited a read on the coffee table. Suits of armor and medieval weapons—museum-quality swords, spears, and daggers—graced the walls. The frosty beer, setting on the table, sweated in wait.

***

Bruce ripped a shirt off the hanger and grabbed his Glock, shoving it inside his waistband at the small of his back. He walked into the master suite bath, turned on the sink's tap, and stared at his cell phone. A few moments later, he exited the bathroom to join Jennifer.

"May I use your bathroom, Bruce?" Jennifer called out.

"Of course," he responded with a smile.

In the guest bathroom, Jennifer turned on the tap and opened the medicine cabinet. *Hmmm . . . Band-Aids, eye drops, Benadryl, Hydrocodone, and Marplan . . . Ah, Marplan, my friend.*

Popping the cap, she grabbed a few pills, crushed them on the counter with a bottle of cough syrup, poured the powder into a Kleenex tissue, and folded it several times before pocketing it—a treasure chest in case of trouble.

When Jennifer returned to the living room, Bruce greeted her with a grin.

"We should take separate cars," he suggested, "so that one of us has a chance of escaping." While laughing at his own wicked sense of humor, Bruce held the front door open for her, inviting her onward with a wave. "I'll lead the way, since I know where he lives. Actually, I had to take a check by his house recently for a busted poker table courtesy of our brawling kids," Bruce chuckled.

Before she started her car, Jennifer checked her phone for messages.

Why would I expect anything more than no coverage here?

After slamming her phone into the drink holder, she proceeded to follow Bruce.

***

"Just take me to Jennifer's, Max," Camille said with a frown. "As much as I love technology, I hate it," she added staring at her phone in dismay. "How can you stand that hissing noise?"

"People adapt to all sorts of job challenges. You know that," he replied.

Camille stuck her tongue out at him before turning around in her seat. Her jaw dropped when she saw the guns in the backseat, positioned upright and ready for use. "Wow! Those guns in the backseat—what are they? AK-47s?"

"They're my friends. They can be your friends if you learn to shoot. As someone said, 'God made man and God made woman, but Sam Colt made them equal,'" he answered with a smile.

"I know how to shoot a shotgun," she answered with an upward tilt of her head.

"Semiautomatics require less reloading—an advantage in my line of work," he said.

"Maybe you'll be fortunate enough to teach me to shoot one of those guns."

"Maybe . . ." he smiled.

"And maybe I'll be better than you," Camille beamed.

"Well, Cami, if any one person would be better than I am, I hope it's you," Max muttered.

"Charm is a disarming weapon," Camille said, blushing.

"Yes, I know," Max said with a smirk.

"Changing the subject—do you always keep that damn scanner on?" she quizzed.

"I love my work, Cami," he emoted with a grand gesture of his arm, an opera singer reaching out to the audience while singing an aria not more grandiose.

"What do you—" Camille began.

"Unit 1398, I have a 1050—three vehicles, a SUV and two

motorcycles with injuries at CR 419 bridge," the scanner interrupted.

"Wait . . . you don't think . . ." Camille said, shuddering.

"I think we can breeze by for a quick look. Is it nearby?" Max asked.

"Yes."

"It's possible, but it's also just as likely that someone else is involved," Max said, patting her hand. "Now, tell me the quickest way to get there."

***

Gordon walked outside to get his police scanner when he noticed two cars traveling along his driveway. With rattlesnake quickness, he drew a gun from his shoulder holster.

"Unit 1398, I have a 1050—three vehicles, a SUV and two motorcycles with injuries at CR 419 bridge. EMS and Fire en route," the dispatcher alerted.

Transfixed, he craned his neck to look back at the scanner. Robotically, he refocused on the driveway.

Jennifer and Bruce parked next to one another and exited their cars about the same time. "Damn it all!" Jennifer cursed as her car keys fell from her hand onto the gravel driveway. In a flash, she folded herself in half to retrieve them.

"Is he acting strange or what?" Bruce commented as they walked toward the outdoor patio furniture.

"For Gordon, the only strange behavior is kindness or good-heartedness," Jennifer hissed as she balled her fists, ready to punch.

Gordon sat at the black wrought-iron table, his gun pushed off to the side. He grabbed his cell phone and speed-dialed Grant's number. With a wince, he watched Jennifer and Bruce pull out chairs to sit in.

"Why don't you help yourselves?" he snapped. "Why are you here?"

"We can't reach Camille or Ben or Grant," Jennifer explained.

"And this is my problem because . . . ?" he uttered, lacing his hands together.

"Have you talked to Grant within the last hour?" Bruce inquired.

"No—no I haven't," Gordon answered. "A better question would be . . . why was Ben tracking Grant at the motel this morning?"

"Wh . . . at! What do you mean?" Bruce asked in wide-eyed astonishment.

"Why was Grant at the motel this morning? What was he doing there? Why would Camille be with him at a motel earlier today?" Jennifer quizzed.

Gordon stood up slowly and turned toward the front door.

"I asked you a question, Gordon. Now, I'll ask again differently. Do you know where our kids are?" Jennifer snarled.

Turning around to face her, Gordon blushed. He gritted his teeth in anger. "Remember who you're talking to, Jennifer. That's a warning—unless you want me to put you in your place, woman," he barked, aiming a make-believe gun at her.

In a flash, Jennifer stood up and said, "Oh, yes, you mean the public servant, the corrupt cop, refuses to help me? Are you threatening me?" She laughed and continued, "Yes, Gordon only helps himself to whatever he can, whatever isn't bolted to the floor."

"True, your newfound daughter felt bolted to the floor a time or two. It was quite enjoyable for me, actually. She fought the first couple of times; after that, she figured out she had to choose between being beaten and raped or just raped. She finally learned the program," he chuckled.

"You pedophile piece of shit!" Jennifer screamed as she stepped toward him, hurling a fistful of gravelly dirt into his face—microdermabrasion for his myopia.

Stumbling toward her while wiping his eyes, he raged, "I'll make you beg to die, you slut."

"Not today, Gordon, because today is my day. My day to put the hurt on you," she said as she stepped back and pulled the lipstick from her front pocket. With a flip of her finger, the cap arced acrobatically in the air before the torturous stream struck his eyes with fire-hose force.

Gordon crumpled in front of them, convulsing like an epileptic in the throes of a seizure.

As Jennifer watched him writhe in agony, she said, "Well, Bruce, you're at a crossroads. You can do the right thing or the wrong thing. I'm sure it's scary to take sides against Gordon. What'll it be—fight me, or join me to find our kids? If Gordon hadn't been pimping out Camille, we wouldn't be standing here. Ben probably wouldn't be tracking Grant to kick his ass. I saw that bible on the coffee table, Bruce. Do you want to be the stand-up guy or not? Would Ben want you to help the guy who raped his longtime love? I can tell you what Ben would say. What do you say?"

"I say—" Bruce began.

"Unit 1398 requesting assistance at CR 419 bridge. Backup required."

"We should go there, just to be sure," Jennifer muttered. "Let's leave this shit on the ground and go!" she urged.

"Yes, yes I definitely agree," Bruce said, averting her gaze.

***

"Do you think you were successful with two bars?" Sophia asked.

"The reception was spotty, but I think she heard me most of the time," Ethan replied. "In the meantime, we have to sit here and wait for the infantry."

"Good God! What do you think happened here?" Sophia asked as she crossed her arms in front of her chest.

"I think someone flamed. You know—became psychotic. Maybe someone passed too close, or drove too slow, or miscalculated the best time to merge with traffic. From the angle of that rupture in the guard railing, the pregnant mom crossed into the opposing lane of traffic either by overcorrecting or by trying to buy some time to gain control," Ethan replied.

"Some people say that no one wants to forgive another driver's mistakes; the error becomes an injustice, a personal affront. With all of the injustice in the world that many feel helpless to correct, retaliation provides immediate gratification, a way to right a wrong right now. Anyone can rage—if you have emotions, you can rage. I think rage claimed a mom and her kids today. Three families lost their kids today in a game of asphalt hijinks. Who won today?" Sophia bawled. "Who can claim that they reached their destination first?" Smearing her tears away with her hand, she spat, "*After all being first being fast trumps the risk of injuring or killing people.*"

Chapter 20
Watley

"I'm not getting out of this car in my pajama tank top and shorts unless I have to. I had to eat in a restaurant like this," Camille complained as they rushed to the accident scene.

"Probably a good idea, since you'd be another reason for gawkers to stop and look," Max continued. "But I see girls in the grocery stores shopping in their pajamas. You shouldn't worry."

When Max and Camille located the 419 bridge, Max immediately spotted a man and a woman sitting near the battered car. Looking beyond the couple, he stared at the heap of bodies. He turned to talk to Camille when he heard the *click* of her seatbelt. She vaulted in a flash. He watched as she navigated the embankment in her cowboy boots, all but surfing down the hill, and he knew . . . knew they had found Grant and Ben.

"Oh my God! They're dead, both of them," she screamed as she melted into the ground. Sophia rushed to her side to comfort her, holding her like a young child.

Max studied the bodies from one side, then the other.

"It looks a double suicide. One death can be a catalyst for another," Max analyzed out loud.

"What can we do?" Camille managed to shout, struggling

between sobs.

"Nothing, just wait for more help," he answered coolly while watching a man approach.

"The car contains more victims, including children," Ethan said as he stood by Max's side.

"From the looks of the car and the drop, they must all be dead or near death," Max concluded.

"Yes," Ethan whispered.

"Excuse me while I assess the scene," Max said.

When Camille glanced up again, she saw Jennifer and Bruce sliding down the steep embankment. While she felt relieved to see Jennifer, she winced at the thought of Bruce on the scene. He always acted too interested in her.

Looking away, she tried to remember if there was a single moment when she had labeled Bruce as a foe.

"Oh, how horrific!" Jennifer screamed. "Ben dead, Grant dead, and . . ." she muttered as her eyes traveled to the car. She turned away from Camille's open arms, bent at the waist, and retched.

"My son shouldn't be dead! Grant acted like he owned the roads because his dad could weasel him out of any situation, but my boy was safe, smart, and kind. I'll find out why this happened, and someone will pay!" Bruce yelled as his fists balled and uncoiled in growing indignation. "What can you tell us about this, Camille? You bear some responsibility for this by throwing yourself at these boys," he proclaimed as he stuck an accusatory finger in her face.

"Wait just a minute here, Bruce. You need to back off—or should I back you off with one of my many tools?" Jennifer hissed as she approached him.

"Everyone, take a breath. I'm in charge of this scene until the sheriff arrives," Max announced, stepping between justice-seeking Jennifer and belligerent Bruce.

"And who the hell are you?" Bruce asked.

"I'm the man in charge. Do you want to fight me for the title? I know you're grief-stricken, but I won't let you attack anyone," Max said with a steely stare.

"Hey, you're in charge. It's not that important to me," Bruce replied.

"I didn't think so," Max answered with a smile.

***

As the sirens and red lights approached, Bruce stood weeping near the body of his son.

Camille, Sophia, and Jennifer huddled together, arms wrapped from shoulder to shoulder, to comfort one another.

"I bet Grant caused this. His dad made him King of the Roads around here. He was bulletproof because Daddy would always fix his mistakes," Jennifer said. "Heck, I remember Grant ran some poor woman off the road a couple of years ago. She lost control of her car and hit a pylon, dying instantly, they say. Grant called his dad. There were many witnesses. Out-of-state relatives talked about a lawsuit—at least until the discovery of illegal drugs in her car, and the discovery that she was heavily in debt. But her family said she didn't even like to take drugs for legitimate reasons. She favored Eastern medicine. I certainly never heard any talk about her. By working with the youth group, I heard talk about the users. In our small town, I would know."

Biting her lip, she continued, "I'll never forget seeing that accident. I'll never forget how cold Grant was about it. That poor woman wouldn't pull over for him. But the newspaper reported that apparently a black widow bite on her hand sent her into panic mode to reach a doctor."

Ethan and Max sat together, comparing notes on the why and the how.

When the police cars parked, Worth County Sheriff Watley, a tall, stern man sporting a gray buzz cut, exited his car, slamming the door. As all eyes followed the sheriff, the passenger door opened to reveal that Gordon rode shotgun.

An ambulance pulled up behind Watley's squad car.

Gordon skidded and skated down the hill for a closer look. "My boy! My son can't be dead!" he wailed, squatting next to Grant's body.

Watley patted his back, then walked closer to the wreck of the SUV. After peering into the car, he grimaced and ran his hand over his hair. "Can anyone tell me what happened here? Are there any witnesses?"

"No, we don't think so," Ethan answered.

"And who would you be?" Watley asked.

"My wife and I happened upon this wreck. Everyone was dead when we arrived," Ethan said.

"Anyone else have anything to add? Okay. I want everyone to wait for me at my squad car up the hill, where I'll gather statements. Let's give Gordon and Bruce a few minutes alone with their boys." Looking first at the group, then at his clipboard and forms, Watley shouted, "Now!"

A paramedic raced to Watley's side. With a quick shake of his head, he conveyed his assessment of the situation. Watley put on latex gloves to investigate, careful to snap each finger for a perfect fit.

With the speed of pack mules moving uphill, the cluster of people followed Watley's orders—all except Jennifer, who lagged behind, feigning compliance.

Sophia peeked over her shoulder to see Watley and the paramedic talking outside the SUV. Watley rested his clipboard against the car as he continued to talk. With a wave of his hand, Watley dispatched the paramedic to begin body removal.

Max and Camille reached the squad car first.

"What do we tell them? I mean, you don't want to blow your cover. Do you?" Camille questioned.

"No, we'll tell them . . . that I'm your boyfriend," Max replied.

"And your name is?" Camille quizzed.

"Max. bossy, big-hearted Max, who likes to be the leader," he said with a hint of a smile.

"And what address will you give?" Camille persisted.

"I actually have a post office box—" Max began.

"The ring! Where's my boy's ring?" Gordon yelled, holding Grant's hand and examining it before reaching for the other. "It's gone! Maybe Ben has it!" He glared at Bruce before his eyes and hands started to search.

"Get your hands off my son! I'll look!" Bruce shouted, pushing Gordon aside.

"Did you forget who the fuck *I* am?" Gordon roared.

"My son, my search. Do you want to fight about this?" Bruce growled.

"Look, fellas, I'll look," Curt, the paramedic, intervened. With great care, he checked one hand, then the other. "No ring on either hand."

"Grant lost that ring in a poker game, Gordon. You know that!" Bruce shouted.

"I gave him that ring. He should have it. Maybe your boy cheated him out of it," Gordon accused.

"Don't call my son a liar!" Bruce yelled again, wrath embedded in his fury-filled eyes.

Watley approached, swinging a slender black baton. His annoyed expression signaled his intentions as he moved closer to the unsuspecting pair.

"Shut up, Bruce!" he shouted before slamming his baton across the middle of his back.

Bruce yelped and folded like a cheap lawn chair before falling to the ground.

"What the fuck! Why hit me? He was the aggressor," Bruce whined.

"From where I stood, you were the problem. Isn't that right, Curt?" Watley asked.

Camille felt the momentary squeeze of Max's hand as they stood transfixed.

"Yeah, I agree, Sheriff. In fact, maybe, you should convince—" Curt said with a smile.

"Wait! Gordon, I have the ring on my finger," Jennifer yelled, pointing at it. Stepping closer, she continued. "The ring that you gave to Grant belonged to my husband. Somebody took it from him when he was killed. Do you know who would do that, Gordon? Rumors have been circulating for years that you were robbing people at accident scenes. From what I hear, you were the first to show up on site. What a coincidence, huh? I bet Sheriff Watley didn't know the ring was missing."

"Woman, you'd better watch yourself!" Gordon spat, his reddening face frozen in fury.

"Is that a threat, Gordon? Because if it is, several people heard what you said," Jennifer challenged.

Sheriff Watley looked at Gordon, his fingers twitching on the baton grip.

"Shut up, Jennifer!" Sheriff Watley ordered. "Wait for me by the car. Bruce, go stand with the others while I have a few words with Gordon."

As Bruce began his climb, Sheriff Watley leaned in to Gordon and whispered, "I know you want to kill her, but I don't want any part of that. Remember, she's smarter than you. Give her credit for knocking you on your ass. Sometimes you should just let it go. You've done this before on a bigger scale. You can do it again."

"The difference is humiliation. I don't want this situation stewing in my gut like yesterday's food poisoning. I need to deal with that bitch and Camille right away," Gordon hissed.

Chapter 21
The Discovery

"And you are who?" Sheriff Watley asked as Gordon stood beside him.

"My name is Max. I'm Camille's boyfriend."

Gordon laughed, stopping when Max glared at him.

"In our small town, everyone knows everyone else's business. Why haven't I heard of you before?" Watley asked.

"Well, maybe Gordon can answer that question. He knows me," Max responded with a dirty grin.

When Watley looked at him, Gordon muttered, "Errrr . . . well, we've done some business together."

Watley tilted his head to the side, looked at the road, then back at Max before asking, "Why would you happen to be in this area, stranger?"

"I decided to see a little more of the countryside with my darling date, Camille. She said people frequently travel this road."

"And Camille, what do you have to say?" Watley quizzed.

"I have nothing to add," Camille said.

"Did you see the wreck occur, Max?" Watley inquired.

"No, but I think I know what happened," Max offered.

"Is that right?" Watley leaned in to hear every word and see every physical nuance.

"Yes, one or both of these boys caused this woman to run off the road," Max said.

"And..." Watley pressed.

"For some reason, they died by gunshot wound, maybe self-inflicted, maybe not. I think they knew the victims and that fact became the catalyst for their deaths," Max said.

"That's a smart and precise observation, stranger," Watley commented while stroking his chin.

Silence filled the air, the tension as palpable and visible as the sight of an out-of-control eighteen-wheeler.

"What do you do, anyway?" Watley questioned.

"I'm studying to be a detective at night. By day, I work as an accountant," Max answered.

Watley took a moment to reassess Max again with a vertical stare. "Ok..."

Without saying a word, Sophia handed over her driver's license to Watley.

"Sophia from Austin. Did you see the accident occur?" Watley asked.

"No, we happened to drive by on the way to visit a relative in Nickel. I gave you two licenses—one for me and one for my spouse, Ethan," Sophia said.

Ethan observed as she took charge, and opted to stand beside her quietly.

"What do *you* think occurred?" Watley asked.

"I agree with Max's assessment of the accident. And I think that that jackass, Gordon, knows more than he has shared. Gordon is guilty of something," Sophia accused.

Watley sniffed and spat, looking at the road.

Gordon winced as if he'd been slapped, while Jennifer laughed loudly.

"I'd like for you and all of the folks here to complete and sign an affidavit that will be mailed to you," Watley said as he handed out documents.

"Wait! Aren't you going to interrogate Gordon about Jennifer's allegations? After all, you've been asking all of us questions—all of us except him," Sophia questioned. "Surely, you hold him accountable for his actions, his threats, and potential culpability with her ring."

Watley squeezed the baton more firmly, as evidenced by his throbbing jugular vein. With a glaring stare, he faced her. After rhythmically striking the palm of his hand several times with his baton, he said, "Don't *you* worry, little lady, about how I do *my* job."

"I won't worry about your job, but I will mention Jennifer's comments in my report, and I will keep a copy. And of course, I won't overlook Gordon's actions. Full disclosure, right, Sheriff?" Sophia persisted.

A smile formed on his face as he spun on his heel, parked his baton on his belt, and waved her away like an annoying mosquito.

Gordon stood frowning, glaring first at Sophia, then Jennifer. After a few moments of looking at the bridge, he rushed to join the sheriff in his car.

As Sophia lunged forward to follow, Ethan wrapped one arm around her waist, cupped her mouth, and pulled her away.

Jennifer approached Ethan's car as they prepared to leave. "Thanks, gal, for being outspoken, although you haven't done any favors for yourself or Ethan," she said as she cast her eyes at the ground.

"I've learned to read people. Gordon couldn't be more devious. He's a poisonous snake collaborating with the sheriff in some way. You must be cautious about your safety and that of your family.

Vicious doesn't begin to describe him. Always remember to trust your instincts, and you will not fail, but prevail. If y'all need to leave town, call me," she said, scribbling her number on the back of a fast-food receipt. She gave it to Jennifer before Ethan revved the engine to speed away.

***

Max and Camille sat speechless in his white SUV as they traveled back to Camille's house. Camille's sobs drowned out any thought of conversation.

Max adjusted the rearview mirror, then he covered Camille's hand with his own.

"I need to stay with you and Jennifer at the house from now on," Max muttered.

"Okay. I'd like that. All of us would like that," Camille whispered.

"Do you have a lot of ammo?" Max asked.

"Not a lot. We should buy some more," Camille said.

"My thoughts, exactly. We need to switch cars. I'll go into town after I leave you at Jennifer's. You pick up Joy and wait for me to return. If the eyes in town are on watch, I want them focused on me," Max plotted.

"Yes—Jennifer, you, I, and Joy all under the same roof. I like that plan," Camille said with a sigh.

***

Jennifer followed Bruce to his house, parked her car, and walked over to his car to offer her condolences.

"My deepest sympathies for your loss," she said, standing at his open window.

Bruce looked away and wiped his tears. "Thank you. I loved him more than anyone or anything. Why would he take his own life?"

"I'd reserve judgment until you read the accident report. By the way, thanks for joining me on the search," Jennifer added.

"I owe you a debt of thanks for stepping up about that ring," he said as climbed out of his vehicle. When he pushed the door shut behind him, she saw *it*—a long scar that began at his wrist and extended beyond his elbow.

"May I call in that debt by asking for an icy glass of water? The nearest convenience store is off my route to return home, and I'm parched from standing out in the sun," Jennifer said, looking into his eyes.

"Absolutely. I'm thirsty, too. A glass of sweet tea would suit me just fine," Bruce chuckled. "Guess I'm more Southern than I realize."

Inside the house, Jennifer walked into the kitchen and spun around. "Tell you what. Why don't I get the drinks while you change your shirt? If you're like me, you must be covered in sweat."

"I'd be happy to get the drinks for us, but a shirt change and a splash of aftershave would make me less smelly," Bruce smiled.

"If you don't mind loaning a clean shirt to me also, I'd appreciate it. I promise to return it clean to your front door," Jennifer asked.

"Okay. The sweet tea is in the green plastic pitcher, and the refrigerator dispenses cold water and ice cubes from the door. Be back in a few minutes," Bruce said as he dashed out of the room.

Jennifer opened the refrigerator, located the pitcher, and grabbed two glasses from the shelves near the sink. Moving back to the refrigerator, located on the right side of the kitchen nestled next to a row of cabinets, she glanced toward the hallway leading to the bedroom and bath. She patted her back pocket and reached for the folded tissue tucked in there. As she poured its contents into the sweet tea, she kept her eyes on the hallway.

"No spoon! I forgot to get a spoon," she whispered to herself. Jamming her index finger into the glass, she stirred.

"Why, you don't even have a glass of water yet!" Bruce commented as he approached.

"Mommy mindset always on—raising a child requires a different thought process, as you know. Look after others first," she said with a semi-smile as she added crushed ice from the refrigerator.

"Here you go. Now, I'll enjoy that glass of water."

"Do you always put your fingers in drinks?" Bruce crossed his arms and leaned against the counter.

"Yeah, well, I thought I might drink the tea instead, but it didn't taste sugary enough. Instead of looking for the sugar and a spoon, I tried to stir the sugar settled in the bottom of the glass. Like I said—very thirsty."

"I believe you, even though it's a bit unsanitary for my tastes," he said, glancing at the empty pitcher sitting on the countertop. "I'll take care of your water request. Maybe we can move to the living room, where it's more comfortable. I dropped a clean shirt on the loveseat for you."

"Of course, thanks," she said as she pivoted away from him and moved toward the living room.

"Never mind! *You* stay *here* with me!" He lunged at her, putting one arm around her waist and cupping her mouth with a cloth. "Yes, it's better if you shut up and stay here with me."

When Jennifer's eyes rolled back into her head, and her body went limp, Bruce dragged her into another room.

Bruce placed her on his bed. He opened his nightstand drawer, where his hands searched for something important. He continued to keep his eyes trained on Jennifer.

"Ah . . . There it is . . ."

His hands found the sought-after prize—the mask. Putting it on the nightstand, he walked into the kitchen to reclaim his glass of tea. Returning to the room, he sat on the bed next to Jennifer. Jennifer's long, brown hair framed her heart-shaped face. Her curvy body, covered by a yellow cotton sundress, suddenly twitched. With a smile, Bruce pushed a lock of hair behind her ear before proceeding to drink his tea.

Chapter 22
Karma

The afternoon sun was beginning to hide behind the horizon when Gordon returned home without his son. Watley arranged for one of his friends to deliver Grant's bike to Gordon that day. Gordon peeked out of the curtains when the bike arrived. He stared at the high school graduation gift to his son, wishing he could turn back time. He gripped the curtains and thrashed them together like cymbals before walking across the living room to stand in front of the antique armoire that had been converted to a bar. After he opened the doors, he noticed that the bottles of liquor required a good dusting, but the contents required only the turn of a cap to be enjoyed. And that's exactly what Gordon decided to do—for the next couple of hours, anyway.

***

Gordon watched the sun disappear from sight as he tipped back the bottle once again. After he turned on the porch light, he walked outside, sat in a lawn chair, and stared at Grant's bike.

How fitting! Grant's bike will carry me to the kill zone. Grant, my pride and joy, how can I go on without you? This is Camille's fault! Her actions caused this! Camille and Ben. Ben couldn't stand in the way of my son getting the job done, doing as I asked. I know it would've been different if not for Camille. And Jennifer, a woman with a big mouth—a mouth that can cause me more problems.

Gordon sobbed, wiped away his tears, and walked to the bike, wielding a bottle. He sat down on the iron horse, placed the bottle between his legs, strapped on a spare helmet to honor an agreement with his son, and started the engine. Another swallow before he tossed the bottle into the rose bushes, and he was ready to meet the road.

***

Gordon pushed the bike, passing car after car. The speed limit posed no constraints for *him*. He beamed as he considered the punishment he'd heap on Camille and Jennifer. He raced faster along the road, topping out at 100 miles per hour in the dark. An exit ramp ahead could mean only a quicker arrival.

He veered onto the ramp, only to hit a pothole. In an instant, the Rain County sheriff, the grieving father, became a missile built of flesh and bone rocketing through the night air.

"Hellllllllll . . . p!"

His body flew forward like a Tomahawk launched until his upper neck collided with one of several gold concrete guard posts, stationed like sentries to protect and serve. The snap of a twig could not be more facile than the forward momentum and concrete post which partnered to sever Gordon's head from his body. In a flash, the helmet-covered head rolled down the ramp to rest against a golden pylon.

***

After Max dropped her off at Jennifer's house, Camille drove to Rose's house to bring Joy home. She knew everyone would feel better when all loved ones converged under the same roof—no wondering, no worrying about *that*, anyway. She called Rose to warn her that she'd be driving a white Dodge Durango SUV with tinted windows.

"Where's your car?" Joy asked as she bounded into the car.

"Max and I switched cars today. He wanted to drive the Corvette," she answered, almost mumbling.

"Where's Mom? Did you find Ben?"

"Jennifer should be home soon," Camille replied, exactly as she had rehearsed. No need to worry Joy, she thought. "Ben . . . I don't want to talk about Ben," Camille said as her thoughts silenced her voice. The tears began to flow, and she smeared them away just as quickly as they appeared. "In fact, I don't want to talk about anything until we reach the house."

***

Bruce enjoyed his conquest before taking Jennifer's cell phone, wrapping her in his bathrobe, and tying her to a chair. His glass of tea sat on the nightstand, sweating. Bruce's lust was greater than his thirst, so the glass remained mostly full. The bruises and fingerprints on Jennifer's wrists and neck reminded him of tattoos—tattoos for his pleasure made by his hands. He chuckled as he positioned her to face his bedroom mirror.

She'll know I took her by the pain she'll feel sitting on her ass. I'll bet the pain in her crotch can't compare. When you wake, Miss Pretty, you will see some of the liberties I did take.

He showered, dressed, and grabbed his tea before settling into his car to drive to another house to satiate his libido with another woman—the one responsible for his son's demise. He giggled as a single thought raced across his mind: Jennifer won't be home.

Chapter 23
The Epiphany

Bruce recognized Grant's bike as he approached the ramp, the custom paint job unmistakable, even on a crumpled piece of iron. Someone slumped near the bike on the side of the road with his back toward him.

Shit! That must be Gordon! He wouldn't let anyone else ride that bike!

After parking his car, he grabbed a flashlight from his glove box and exited to investigate. His eyes scanned the landscape for clues or activity. He stood next to the body for a brief moment before he pulled back a shoulder to look for signs of life.

Gordon! Nooooooo . . . !

Transfixed by the horror, Bruce pivoted and spotted the helmet. The lenses of the eyes reflected the light back at him like a demon in a bad dream.

Oh my God!

After running at breakneck speed toward his car, Bruce arrived at his driver door winded. A gulp of air later, he opened his door, vaulted in and sped away. The helmeted head jostled out of position and rolled after him.

***

To call 911 or not? I think not. I've got better things to do.

Bruce drove by the front of Jennifer's house, noting that the living room lights were on. At 10:30 p.m., the house looked lit up for a party.

Heck, they could stay awake all night long.

To forge a plan, Bruce drove around the sleepy neighborhood. It reminded him of the fairgrounds after the final day of festivities—deserted, quiet and dark. When he saw the empty lot behind Jennifer's house, he knew he would begin there.

***

Camille paced the floor of the living room, clenching her fists with every step. Jennifer hadn't returned home. Her voice mail answered Camille's countless calls.

Max pulled into the driveway. After he exited the car, he leaned back into the cab, grabbed his semiautomatic rifle, cradled it in his arms to insure it wouldn't be scratched, stepped back for clearance and then slung it over his shoulder. Circling around to the passenger side, he plucked a big bulky bag from the passenger side floorboard.

Camille peeked out of the curtains before running to Max's side to claim his strength and swagger. Slipping her arm around him, she blurted out: "I'm scared to death. Jennifer isn't here. I've called her several times."

Max wiggled out of the arm lock to look into her eyes. He held her hand with his free hand, and squeezed it tightly. "That's not good. Where do we start?"

"I'm not quite sure, but she told me she planned to follow Bruce home."

"Okay, you stay here with Joy, and I'll take your car to Bruce's. Now, all I need is an address or directions," Max said.

"You know, that guy Bruce creeps me out. It's like I know him as more than Ben's dad," Camille said she rubbed her forehead. "The long scar on his arm," she muttered. "That weird, unmistakable scar," she continued. "Wait a minute! . . . I know! I know!"

"What! For God's sake, tell me, Cami!"

She shuddered before she said, "He's the one in the porn video—the sadist, wearing a mask. He abused me when I was drugged."

"Is that right?" Max barked as his jaw flexed in fury.

"I'm very frightened for Jennifer's safety. Please leave now. And, Max, no punishment would be too horrible for him."

Chapter 24
Bee Smart

Bruce turned down the quiet, dark street behind Joy's house once again to strengthen the fabric of his plan. As he approached the empty lot, he could see Max backing into the street in Camille's Corvette; the outdoor lighting, once a curse, was now a blessing. He continued to inch along, using the trees for cover.

A fringe of trees, a herd of horses, a barn to hide in. Perfect!

Bruce parked his car behind the empty lot, out of the line of sight from the house. With flashlight in hand, he crawled into the corral. The crackling of dead leaves and branches under his boots made Bruce cringe with every step.

The guard horse, Trooper, noticed him from the first moment. He stood and stared, and the other horses followed suit.

I hate horses.

He picked up a rock and hurled it at Trooper, who had started to walk toward him. Trooper spun on his back leg, bucked and kicked out with both hooves, triggering the motion-sensor lighting. Trooper called to the horses to alert them about the presence of a bad stranger. The horses scattered like pebbles. Another rock, another miss, and Bruce entered the barn and closed the door.

Indoors, Camille locked all the doors in the house and holstered her cell phone. She and Joy decided to station themselves in Jennifer's bedroom with the ammo. Camille and Joy loaded gun after gun side by side.

"Our armory isn't complete without the crossbow and arrows," Camille decided. "More is more. If you have an extra gun, Joy, please get it."

"We'd have more, but Mom stashed some guns in her car. When will she be home? I worry about her," Joy whined.

"Trust Max to find her. He has a talent for finding people," Camille reassured.

"Yeah, he found you. I'm going to get my archery stuff now," Joy said.

Joy stopped in her tracks when she saw the corral and barn area illuminated. A flash of color blurred by as Trooper galloped underneath the lighting. In fact, almost all outdoor lights had switched on as if to display a herd in flight.

"What about the crossbow?" Camille asked with her back turned to the window. Joy averted her gaze by focusing on the horses. She shifted her weight from one foot to the next while Camille loaded a shotgun.

"Yeah, I'll go get it, but I want to grab a snack afterward. I'm really hungry."

***

After Joy delivered the crossbow and arrows, she quietly slunk out the back door, toting her personal pink shotgun. She listened and watched the horses, knowing that a stranger lurked nearby. She had learned that horses could smell strangers in a barn or corral. She formed a plan and began to put it into play, as a target, by whispering it to herself:

"Shoot *around* the horses. Fire a warning shot to get Camille's attention and scare away the stranger."

Aiming at the tallest tree to the left of the corral, she fired once.

When Camille heard the shot, she turned to the French doors and opened them. She saw Joy turn toward the window and wave. At the same moment, she saw a silhouette rush through the corral toward Joy.

"Joy, someone is behind you! Run, now! Run, Joy, run!" Camille screamed.

"Heeeeeelp! I'm scarrrrrred!" Joy yelled.

"Keep running! Don't look back! I'll protect you!" Camille coached.

Joy screamed again, stumbled, and dropped her gun.

Can't use a shotgun because of the spray of buckshot. Joy could be hit.

Camille's eyes darted around the room for an answer. She grabbed the crossbow and arrow.

"You can't escape, little girl. You escaped your awful daddy Gordon, but you can't escape me!" he taunted as he chased.

"You're a liar!" she slowed to turn and shout.

"Ignore him, Joy!" Camille demanded as she aimed.

"Little Joy, fathered by Gordon. But you still fared better than Camille. Right, Camille? I spared you and Grant once, when Purvis died. I won't spare you this time," Bruce shouted, only a few steps away from Joy.

"Faster, Joy, and hit the dirt!" Camille screamed.

The arrow traveled an arc toward a large tree, the reach of its long limb extending beyond the corral. The first arrow missed the mark but impaled Bruce's shoulder. He yelped in agony as he continued his pursuit.

Camille reloaded and adjusted with deadly intent, her next choice clear. Aiming much higher, the arrow struck the bull's-eye.

The transient bees that considered this hive home for two months lived comfortably and peacefully near the uninterested horses. The arrow intrusion perceived as a predator, any fast movement close to the hive perceived as the culprit.

"Just to be sure," she mumbled as she grabbed the ready shotgun, aimed, and fired at the impaled hive. After she racked the shotgun, she zeroed in on Mark's bees, nestled in their cozy chest-of-drawers habitats. A deep breath and an exhale later, she blasted the target, which exploded into a starburst of flying wood, waxy comb, and a cloud of buzzing, angry bees.

Joy hit the dirt, but Bruce continued to chase until the angry hives swarmed him and covered him, causing him to fall to the ground like a statue toppled. While he swatted and struggled, his screams filled the air. With one sting after another, the attack pheromone released drew more defenders to the malevolent target, the hit man.

"Ohhhh . . . ! Ewww . . . ! The pain is killing me! In my nose, in my ears! Help! My mouth!"

Joy slowly turned to look and froze when a bee buzzed close by. She knew never to swat and never to run.

***

A day had passed since the bees attacked Bruce. Joy, Max, and Camille gathered around the kitchen table as the sun slipped behind the horizon. Jennifer stood in front of the kitchen's bay window, gazing at the horses.

"I'm so happy you're safe and sound, Jennifer," Camille said as she embraced her.

"I'm damaged, but not dead. I guess...I should be grateful that I wasn't awake. After I showered away his pine-disinfectant cologne,

I immediately felt better," she mumbled. She didn't turn, but continued to study the outdoors. "I've thought about this all night long. Trauma, sadly enough, is... sometimes part of life. I can let this crush me or I can rise above it. I'll deal with it my way, but I don't want to talk about it now." Jennifer looked away from the pastoral scene to face her daughter. "Bruce is dead. Karma kills. The bees provided the deadly payback that he earned," Jennifer gloated.

Moments of weighty silence filled the room, as intense as a home invasion. Questions to be asked, questions not to be asked, questions to be avoided clouded the collective conscience.

"I'm not sure this is the best time to discuss this, but Bruce claimed that Gordon is my father. Is that true?" Joy asked softly, her eyes focused on the floor.

"Yes, Mark adopted you, Joy, when you were a baby," Jennifer replied. She reached across the table for Joy's hand.

Joy scowled, yet accepted her touch.

"I left Gordon shortly after you were born with zero regrets. When I met Mark, I knew he was my soul mate." After she squeezed Joy's hand, she continued, "Gordon cared only about having and raising a son. Girls didn't matter to him—even his own daughter would be objectified. He was a misogynist, a woman hater, twenty-four hours a day seven days a week. Bruce, on the other hand, rumored to be misogynistic only when he drank."

"Who is Grant's mom?" Camille asked, sitting back down.

"A high school graduate who tried to make it work, but who eventually died in Gordon's house. It was ruled as a suicide, which everyone accepted. After all, who'd want to cross Gordon? In a small town, everyone seems to know everyone else's business, even the sheriff's business," Jennifer said as she averted her eyes. "Your grandmother was your hero, your patron saint. Your so-called mom and dad heaped abuse on her, but she weathered the storm to keep you out of the line of fire. In fact, if anyone criticized you, well . . . she'd shred them."

"Welcome to my horror," Joy snapped. "Who'd want to be related to Gordon? Ewwww!"

"Let's all take a breath. *All* of us need therapy. *We* survived our encounters with them, so *we're survivors*. In order to be happy survivors, we have to be grateful survivors and be focused on living happy, meaningful lives." She turned Mark's ring on her finger. "Our lives are our message." As the tears wet her face, she hugged Camille and Max.

"Count me in!" Joy squealed as she layered into the group hug.

Chapter 25
The Dance

A year after the apocalypse at and near her home, Camille lay on her stomach on her bed. Wearing a black leather bustier, black fishnet stockings, thigh-high leather boots, and a purple satin Mardi Gras cat mask excited her, but the thought of the evening's events thrilled her even more. It would be the *first* time for both of them to explore their wildest fantasies. Months of therapy led them to this moment, when Camille could stay in the moment and be a demanding diva. With a naughty smile, she stroked the expanse of ocean blue silk sheets as the evening sun breached the sheer curtain barrier one last time before retiring. She hit the play button on the bedside CD player. "Shameless" blasted from the speakers.

"Still waiting and wanting," Camille called out. Reaching under her pillow, she grabbed a horse crop and struck the wall. "You spend more time in the bathroom than Joy."

A turn of the knob, and Max appeared in the doorway, dressed in a pale blue western shirt with black pearl snaps and faded denim jeans adorned with a silver belt buckle. He strutted into the room with his thumbs hooked into the belt loops near his fly. His black boots announced his important arrival. His shoulder-length black hair was pulled back in a ponytail. A black felt cowboy hat perched on his head.

"I can't believe we're finally doing this. Our fantasies fulfilled," he said as his longing gaze rested on her. "I have a gift for you before we start."

"Whhhaaat!" she said as her jaw dropped. "I . . . I don't have a gift for you," she mouthed with a frown.

"Now, just wait, no worries. I wanted this to be a total surprise," he soothed with a smile. "Sit up and close your eyes, Cami."

After she settled in on the corner of the bed, he approached, carrying a little purple velvet box.

"Keep your eyes closed," he said as he took her hand and turned it upward to cup the box. He sat beside her.

"Open your eyes!"

Camille opened the box to find a pair of amethyst teardrop earrings. "Oh! Oh! Gorgeous!" Her eyes misted as she removed them from the case.

"Wait! I want to do this." He combed back her hair to reveal her earlobes. She tried to duck, but he nudged her chin up and planted a chaste kiss on her lips. "You're breathtaking, all of you. I know that, but I want *you* to feel that way about every part of you," he said before he secured the earrings.

When she looked into the mirror, positioned directly across from the bed, she glowed, but at the same time wept. "I feel like the lighthouse in a rainstorm," she giggled.

He hugged her, but she pulled back to cover his mouth with her raging desire. Max allowed a few seconds for the kiss before he turned away.

"Stop, Cami! There's more for us to explore tonight," Max coached before he stood up and extended his hand. "How about a dance with a cowboy, a little two-step, before we unbridle ourselves?"

"Sure, but I'm not sure I can cool off that easily—" she said, slipping her hand in his.

"Control, Cami, for the better bang. We've got a long night ahead. Do you want to take a cold shower and mess up your makeup? I mean, I think you look stunning without it, but it's not *your* way."

"You're right. I'll think 'cold shower' if you keep some distance between our bodies," she acquiesced.

"Okay, let's give it a try."

As they danced around the room, his arm hung over her shoulder while Garth sang "The Dance."

When the music stopped, Max planted a smoldering kiss on Camille's lips and walked to the CD player.

"I'm in the mood for something a little different. Springsteen—perfect. And . . . my favorite song: "Dancing in the Dark," he announced. Facing her with a grin, he said, "Show me your bad girl, Cami." He grabbed the top of the doorframe and leaned toward her, teasingly. "You're in control, Camille. Whatever you want," he said with a wink.

Camille blushed and looked toward the curtains.

"Don't tell me someone stole my sassy vixen!" he teased.

She turned her gaze to him and grinned. "Stand up straight! What's with the hair ties? Let your hair loose. Shake your head and let it fall on your shoulders." With the riding crop that was hidden in the sheets, she stroked the side of his face and smiled before walking to the bed. She paused, facing the wall, before striking her palm with the riding crop. She spun around to face him before settling onto the bed.

"All right, turn around so I can see your ass! Flex your cheeks—one side, then the other, then both. Turn around and run your hands slowly along the length of your body, chest to stomach to thighs," Camille ordered. "Now, turn around and dance for me!" Camille said as she settled onto her stomach, resting her head on her elbows to gawk at the show.

She crossed her legs, ankle over ankle, as she leered. Warmth blanketed her skin like sunshine and warm sand. Her breasts, crotch, and butt burned for his cooling touch. Licking her lips like a cat teased with a trout, she felt the boiling point approach.

Discipline, Camille. Smoke him!

"I want a Chippendale-quality strip! Thrust, pump, and grind your hips. Shake your hair and dance for me! Dance—thrust your hips left and right to the music. Put your hands above your head and clasp them together and thrust your hips—front, center, left, and right. Let's see some skin! Unsnap some of your shirt and unbuckle the buckle! Unzip the zipper a tiny bit! Ooohhh! Wait!" Camille noticed that skin, not cotton, peeked out from his fly. "Stop there!"

She leaped out of bed to stand by him. "Have a seat in that chair," she answered. "Yeah, the blue, high-backed chair near the bed, facing the mirrored triple dresser."

"And?" he questioned.

"Put your hands behind your back, and close your eyes," she instructed.

Camille smiled as she scurried behind him to secure a thin rope around his wrists. She stepped back to admire Mr. Gorgeous Tough Guy, restrained for her to enjoy.

She whistled at him in appreciation.

"Do I look that good with my eyes closed, tied up like a steer?" he joked.

"Well, yes—yes, you do," she marveled as she straddled him. "Eyes closed," she reminded him as she placed her head on his chest and let her hands roam, squeezing the length of his arms and thighs.

When Max squirmed, she laughed. "And how tough are you?"

Max shook his head and cleared his throat.

Switching gears, she grabbed his face in her hands and kissed him until he turned his face away, opening his eyes. "You don't need this!" She snatched his hat, tossing it like a Frisbee onto the bed. She combed her fingers through his hair.

"I'm a wreck. We just got started. Stop!" he begged.

"I'm in charge," she whispered as she tore at his shirt, the snaps popping with abandon. Leaning back, she clawed at his belt buckle and unzipped his fly.

"You're killing me, Camille!" he complained as he peeked over her shoulder at their reflection in the mirror.

"Shut up!" she said as she unsnapped her bustier, tossed it aside, and arched her back to savor her prize.

***

They leaned against one another in sweaty support, breathless from satiating their lust.

"Again! I want to do this again, *now*," Camille whined as she rested her head on his chest.

"Would you mind if I towel off first before we go again?" Wiggling his hands, he began to untie the rope.

"All right," she said with a sigh as she stood up, released him, and put on her bustier.

With a pout, Camille flung herself on the bed and knitted her hands behind her head.

In a few short minutes, Max returned, dressed in a purple silk camisole, matching short shorts, and black UGGs.

"What, no high heels? You surprise me!" she teased.

"I tried those damned torture traps. I like cowboy boots and UGGs. So cushy! What do you think?" he asked as he twirled.

"No makeup?" she asked.

"No, tried that too. It's all about the clothes," Max said as he scratched his forgot-to-shave face. His dark-blue eyes locked on her as he licked his lips. "What a rush! What a relief! I don't feel the pressure to make decisions, to be right, to be in charge."

"Hmmm... purple silk and black sequined UGGs. Never would've envisioned that," she said as she batted her lashes. "You look hot no matter what you wear! How does it feel to wrap yourself in that?"

"Liberating," he announced with a spin. "I always have to win, to be the tough guy, to gamble my life in my job. It helps relieve some of the stress," he said as he strutted toward her.

"This will be good for you, baby," she said as she stood stiletto-tall with her hands on her hips, facing him. "Now, be my slave! Kneel down and lower your head!"

"Yes, ma'am," he said, grateful to have a chance to hide his smirk.

"Nice..." Camille endorsed with a smile.

Max snickered as he looked at the floor. He covered his mouth and coughed to hide his disrespect.

"I approve. You may approach the bed now. You may not meet my gaze," she instructed.

She crossed the room toward him and pressed her body into him. She grazed her hands over the top of the camisole and then reached underneath before raking her nails down his back.

"Oh, my God," Max moaned.

"Control yourself!" Camille commanded, stepping back. "Turn around!"

"I approve!" she said as she popped his ass with the crop. "Now you can share a bed with me. I'll tell you what I want and how I want it. Understood?"

"Yes, ma'am!"

"I'll go to the bed first, and you wait for my orders to approach."

Camille jumped into bed and turned toward the headboard to grab the handcuffs. She snatched the pre-folded navy-blue cotton paisley bandana from the nightstand and placed it under her outstretched thigh.

"Now you may lie on the bed."

Max hurled himself onto the bed playfully and pulled off his UGGs.

"Don't play with me!" she reprimanded.

"Give me those cuffs!" Max said as he cuffed his hands with a quick *click*, raised his arms over his head, and leaned against the headboard.

"What do you have to say for yourself?" she demanded.

"Take me, Cami!" he groaned.

Grabbing the blindfold and securing it, she finished phase one.

Camille climbed on top of him, grabbed his face, and covered his receptive mouth with hers. Pulling away, she kissed his chest. His clean scent drove her wild—the fresh cucumber and melon aroma made her ravenous. When he moaned, she licked and gnawed her way up his muscular arms and back to his mouth again. She pulled away, breathless, as he leaned into her. Leaning back on her hands, she asked, "Max, Max. What will I do with you?"

"Hurt me, Cami. Control me!"

Camille grabbed her crop and stroked the side of his face. "You don't decide to touch me! Do you understand?"

"Yes, Camille. I swear," Max panted.

"Be still and shut up!" Camille commanded.

"Yes ma'am. There's . . . mmmore?" Max stammered.

"Of course, *baby*," Camille cooed. "Now shut up," she ordered as she yanked his shorts off.

Love this! Dominating Mr. CIA!

With a quick vault, she straddled him again and ran her hands through his hair before she bit his bicep and his neck. She sighed and unhooked her bustier, tossing it aside and rubbing against him. After a deep breath, she pawed his biceps—digging in with her nails as she stroked his body with hers. An irritating spark became a roaring flame.

Max began to struggle until she clawed his chest with her long pink nails. Her amethyst and diamond wedding ring glistened, jolted by their gyrations.

"I can't . . . No more!" he wailed.

"But you must . . ." she cajoled. With a squeal of delight, she grabbed his cowboy hat, placed it on her head, and claimed him again like any fierce femme would.

Chapter 26
Going to the Dogs

The morning sun peeked through the sheer curtains to announce the start of a new day. Shards of light spotlighted the sleeping couple partially covered in the blue silk sheets. Handcuffs hung from the bedside lamp, the bustier and crotchless black panties hung from the silent ceiling fan, the black cowboy hat hung from the bedpost, and the UGGs blocked the doorway to the bathroom, one standing and one not.

Camille rustled and wrestled with the sheets so she could rest her head on Max's pillow. She whispered into his ear, "Wake up, Max. Places to go, things to do."

"You want to go somewhere today? You wore me out last night, Cami. I hoped we'd make it a Stop day, as in 'stop everything today to do nothing.' Maybe we could cuddle and watch a movie?" Max suggested as he grabbed her hand to kiss it.

"You should be grateful that I'm not demanding more," she said with a grin as she pulled away. "Now, get up, sleepyhead!" With a smack of her pillow, she made the message very clear.

Camille watched the clock to allow him ten minutes of privacy before she knocked on the door. She smiled as she watched Max brush his teeth wearing only the blue cowboy shirt like a robe.

"Let's shower together! You lather me and I'll lather you," she suggested as she opened the shower door and adjusted the water temperature.

Max's jaw dropped before he spat toothpaste into the sink.

"Really, Cami?"

Camille wrapped her arms around him as he faced the bathroom mirror.

"You're not ninety-nine," Camille said as pulled the shirt off his shoulders and kissed his back. "I'm not asking. I'm telling," she said as she tossed his shirt in the corner. She squeezed his bottom, digging her nails into each cheek as if comparing two cantaloupes simultaneously for purchase. She rubbed her naked body against his back before she let her hands explore his chest, belly and beyond. "We've got more ground to cover, catnip. You shampoo my hair and I'll shampoo yours, then you'll drop to your knees and love me with your luscious mouth."

"No handcuffs, no blindfold?" he asked as he studied her reflection.

"Close your eyes when you step into the shower," Camille answered. "And after all of that, who knows? Maybe, you'll score," Camille teased.

With a wink, she slapped his ass, took his hand, and pulled him into the shower stall.

***

As they inched along the driveway leading up to Jennifer's house, the dogs announced the arrival of a stranger. Camille smiled and squeezed Max's shoulder. The house and surrounding flora didn't reflect the loss of the lion nor the wounded lioness.

In an instant, Jennifer and Joy appeared on the front porch. Jennifer stood to wave while Joy bolted toward the car, followed by

Brewster, the Belgian Malinois.

When the Durango rolled to a stop, Joy attached herself to the door like a barnacle on a ship.

"I'm so happy you're here! You have to come see!"

With a quick pull, she opened the door and invited Camille out with a wave of her hand. When her feet stepped on solid ground, Brewster positioned himself between her and Joy. She stood statue still while he sniffed her hand. In a flash, he leaped up and put his paws on her shoulders to lick her face.

"Oh, Brewster, you're always on guard!" Joy said with a smile as she grabbed Camille's hand to lead her to the back of the house.

Jennifer crossed the front yard to greet Camille and Max with a bear hug.

"What's the big surprise?" Camille asked as Max leaned in closer to hear.

Jennifer pretended to zip her lips as she followed Joy.

As they rounded the corner of house, Camille noticed the backyard had changed; it was now fenced with chain link. When she opened the gate, ten black and tan puppies scrambled toward them like clumsy foals released from a starting gate. Momma dog ran with the pack as they approached the group.

"I'm in love! They're beautiful! Winona is a Momma now!" Camille gushed.

Winona bolted to her and greeted her first with a face-to-face embrace. Camille wrapped her arms around her friend and beamed.

"*Halt!*"

In an instant, Winona sat and awaited the next command as her puppies pounced on her and bit her, treating her like a rubber chew toy offered for entertainment.

"You're so lucky to make money with these amazing animals," Max marveled. "What will they sell for when they're trained?"

"About $12,000 each, plus they'll fight crime in the local communities. From sniffing drugs to tracking for rescue to takedown of thugs, they're multipurpose, with a big bite and a sprinter's speed. We're so proud to be breeders, to be part of the Malinois community," Jennifer boasted as Joy's arm encircled her waist. "Eventually, I plan to become certified to train them."

"We're so lucky that Rose left Brewster to us when she died. Bless her soul!" Joy said with a small smile. "Of course, I'll work with you and Mom on this business until I graduate."

"What happens then?" Max asked.

"I stay, go to college, or join the police force to become a SWAT-team member. I like the SWAT idea best," Joy replied.

"That means you could kick my ass," Camille said.

"That's never been in question," Joy quipped.

"Have any new news, Camille?" Jennifer asked.

"I'm glad you asked. I'm still working with the school outreach to help kids at risk and taking karate lessons. I want to earn my black belt and teach high school girls about self-defense. I read somewhere that one out of every five girls on a college campus will be assaulted. I think I'll call the class 'Self-Defense for University Life.'" Beyond that, I may enroll in college soon to study psychiatry.

"Wow! You as a black belt—that's so hot!" Max sputtered.

"My life is my message, Max," Camille said with a smile as she punched him in the arm.

As the sun rose higher in the east, three belles, several dogs, and a federal agent stood basking in the warmth of the day and in wonder of the bees, as pastel shirts and purple towels on a clothesline danced with the breeze. Three belles—shaped by failure, strengthened by tragedy, carved by circumstances into formidable confident women, cemented into place by triumph—joined hands, grateful that the soft targets had disappeared.

www.ingramcontent.com/pod-product-compliance
Ingram Content Group UK Ltd.
Pitfield, Milton Keynes, MK11 3LW, UK
UKHW021302180426
11947UKWH00015B/978